Glyph

By the same author

Free Love
Like
Other stories and other stories
Hotel World
The whole story and other stories
The accidental
Girl meets boy
The first person and other stories
There but for the
Artful
Shire
How to be both
Public library and other stories
Autumn
Winter
Spring
Summer
Companion piece
Gliff

ali smith
Glyph

HAMISH HAMILTON
an imprint of
PENGUIN BOOKS

HAMISH HAMILTON

UK | USA | Canada | Ireland | Australia
India | New Zealand | South Africa

Hamish Hamilton is part of the Penguin Random House group of companies whose addresses can be found at global.penguinrandomhouse.com

Penguin Random House UK,
One Embassy Gardens, 8 Viaduct Gardens, London SW11 7BW

penguin.co.uk

First published 2026
001

Copyright © Ali Smith, 2026

The moral right of the author has been asserted

No part of this book may be used or reproduced in any manner for the purpose of training artificial intelligence technologies or systems. In accordance with Article 4(3) of the DSM Directive 2019/790, Penguin Random House expressly reserves this work from the text and data mining exception

Every effort has been made to trace copyright holders and to obtain their permission for use of copyright material. The publisher apologizes for any errors or omissions and would be grateful to be notified of any corrections that should be incorporated in future editions of this book

Set in 13/16pt Sabon MT Pro
Typeset by Six Red Marbles UK, Thetford, Norfolk
Printed and bound in Great Britain by Clays Ltd, Elcograf S.p.A.

The authorized representative in the EEA is Penguin Random House Ireland, Morrison Chambers, 32 Nassau Street, Dublin D02 YH68

A CIP catalogue record for this book is available from the British Library

HARDBACK ISBN: 978–0–241–66559–6
TRADE PAPERBACK ISBN: 978–0–241–66561–9

Penguin Random House is committed to a sustainable future for our business, our readers and our planet. This book is made from Forest Stewardship Council® certified paper.

To keep in mind
my fine friend
Paul Bailey

to the courage
of the journalists

for the Bradley-Barleys
with love

and for Sarah Wood
her name written
in every tree

> Politics, for me, is everything that involves
> who gets to do what to whom. That's politics.
> Margaret Atwood

I will briefly demonstrate to you the working principle of a machine under which God Himself would be squashed like a fly. It would reduce a man to the state of blotting paper: a man in boots and spurs, cravat, hat, with his money, jewels, everything.
Honoré de Balzac, trans. Herbert J Hunt

> There was a Young Lady of Norway,
> Who casually sat in a doorway;
> When the door squeezed her flat,
> She exclaimed, 'What of that?'
> This courageous Young Lady of Norway.
> Edward Lear

What do we owe to the dead? 'The work of love in recollecting the one who is dead,' Kierkegaard writes, 'is the work of the most disinterested, free and faithful love.' But it is certainly not the easiest. The dead, after all, not only ask nothing from us, but they also seem to do everything possible in order to be forgotten. This, however, is precisely why the dead are perhaps the most demanding objects of love.
Giorgio Agamben, trans. Kevin Attell

> But the arts do live continuously, and they live literally by faith; their names and their shapes and their uses and their basic meanings survive unchanged in all that matters through times of interruption, diminishment, neglect; they outlive governments and creeds and societies, even the very civilizations that produce them. They cannot be destroyed altogether because they represent the substance of faith and the only reality. They are what we find again when the ruins are cleared away. And even the smallest and most incomplete offering at this time can be a proud act in defense of that faith.
> Katherine Anne Porter

nod

Here's a story our great grandfather kept to himself for most of his life, from back when he was in the Foresters.

Not literal foresters. The Foresters was an army regiment. Our great grandfather when he was a young man enlisted with the Foresters and went to fight in the trenches. Lucky for us he wasn't in the part of the regiment that got sent to Gallipoli and got mostly massacred or we wouldn't be here. Lucky he was only a bit gassed, and lucky he met our great grandmother in the military camp hospital, who didn't know that day she met him that she'd be thumping his back to help him cough up stuff for the rest of his life for the rest of *her* life.

The story goes that our great grandfather, long dead by the time we were born, only ever spoke about his time in that war once, on his deathbed, and only to one of his grandsons who was then aged about eight, who told nobody either till he told his younger sister, our mother, over a decade later when she was nine or ten, and I only know it because a couple of decades after that, when I was about eight myself, she told me a version of it and eventually our uncle also passed on his version. Not to Patch, just to me. Patch was too little and too sensitive at the time to hear this kind of story. But I am as thick skinned as boot leather as our mother used to say.

Anyway, this is what our great grandfather was said to have said.

The person of the best and highest qualities he ever knew in his life was a young man he met in the First World War.

This young man's horse went blind, or one of the horses they had out there did, I don't know now if it was his horse or it was just a horse that happened to be there.

It had been blinded by gas.

The gas had come down, pale yellow, and this type of gas blinded anything with eyes and if it settled on any open skin it burned itself into it. The men – the horses too – would turn a sort of orange colour with the burns the gas gave them and then they'd blister and the blisters it gave them could kill them. At this point in that war the men had masks, and gas masks of a sort for horses existed too but were scarce. This young man saw that the eyes of the horse had turned to eggwhite and he knew they'd have to shoot it, though the horse was otherwise fine, wasn't burnt or blistered, just its eyes that were gone.

So he said to someone, I'm going to take that horse out of this since none of it is of its making.

Which he did.

Later that month they frogmarched him back, the young man, more a boy really; same as our great grandfather he'd probably have been nineteen, maybe twenty, early twenties at the most. Anyway they took him away and the authorities court-martialled him and a general who'd involved himself in the case declared an example should be made. So they did this by roping him to a post early one morning, blindfolding him and having a firing squad shoot him dead.

He'd gone over to the horse and unharnessed it, removed its bridle and let all the leather and metal fall to the ground. Then he'd taken off his own uniform jacket. That's the first thing he did that wasn't allowed. He'd dropped the jacket and its pouches, his gun and his bayonet belt etc on top of the muddy horse tack and he'd taken the horse – it had no bridle or rope on it so what he did was he put his hand to its forehead and took hold of its forelock – away from the place where the encampment was, off in the opposite direction of the noise of the fighting, wherever they were, I don't know where they were, anyway there was woodland still standing somewhere nearby, trees on a patch of land not yet obliterated. He led the blind horse off towards that wood and the horse went with him, it went like a lamb our great grandfather apparently said, though it couldn't see, and the man and the horse went in among the trees and vanished from view.

Afterwards someone told our great grandfather that the young man they shot had been a pit pony boy back in the day down in the mines with his father and his brothers till they'd enlisted.

Here's another story, and it's one that a random person we didn't know and only ever met the once had also kept to herself for most of her life until she decided to tell us.

At least that's what she said when she told us it.

And if that's true, when she did decide to tell anybody, of all people it was two children complete strangers to her she chose to tell it to.

We were at a big family party, a silver wedding celebration for some relatives we didn't know and also never met again held in a hotel in a town I only remember the name of because there was a model village there we were taken to see the next day where we marauded like small giants above the neatness of the streets, the peopleless cottages and miniature grand houses, the little trees and lawns, a church, another church, some more modern looking additions too like shops whose windows you could bend down and peek into and a sign above a door saying Chinese Restaurant.

At one point at this party someone had placed my sister and me in our matching pink dresses one on each side of a very elderly lady and taken a photograph. Then we were left sitting there with her while the grown ups, who'd crowded round to take photos of us and the lady, danced on the dancefloor to a small band up at the end of the room playing old songs, a song about magic moments, a song about anniversary waltzes; I was watching the people going back and fore in each other's arms, even our mother and father were doing it. I'd never seen them dance together before, neither of us had; at home our mother could sometimes hardly walk as far as the end of the garden, but there she was, the same as everyone, smiling and dancing the old fashioned dance in among all the people.

Then I felt the lady we were sitting next to reach and take one of my hands.

I looked down at my hand in her very old looking hand then glanced across her lap as politely as I could at my sister. She was looking back at me in a panic because the very old lady we didn't know had taken one of her hands too.

The lady sat saying nothing, holding our hands quite tightly. When she started to speak her grip, on me at least, tightened even more and continued to tighten as she spoke, so much so that a ring I was wearing was crushed against the finger it was on, painful but I was polite and didn't say.

    She asked us our names. She told us her name. Edie. Then this is what she said,

    there is something I have to tell you both. I hope you can hear me above or through the music, can you?

    I nodded.

    My sister nodded when she saw me nod.

    The old lady nodded back to each of us in turn. Then she said,

    one day, when I was still a young woman, not yet thirty, this was oh way back in the forties, fifty years ago now, I was speeding along on a motorcycle on a country road, it was the south of France. To either side of me there were these very high banks of dried red-brown mud. Probably a tank formation had come this way forcing the earth at the road's edges up on itself, but so high that on both sides it looked like the landscape had been parted like a parting in someone's hair and that I was travelling along that parting.

    At this point we were still at war though the war was nearly over. I'd been sent as go-between for the various allied authorities. You know what I mean by allied? How old are you? And you? Ah. Well. You don't really need to know much, not for this story.

All you need to know is that on this particular day I was carrying confidential intelligence, information, a file of papers that had to be co-signed by some high-uppers then redelivered to the people who'd originally sent me out with them. The papers were very secret. They were particularly important because this information dealt with the end of the war.

I remember it was early evening. It was spring. Very warm and dry the weather after a long wet spell, unseasonably warm now for several days, I remember, and as I came down that road with the mud splayed up and back either side of me I saw something strange ahead, down low, flat to the surface of that road.

It was a shape like a shadow, if a shadow were the opposite of dark. Or a fall of sunlight, if a fall of sunlight were to have no brightness in it.

What I mean is I could tell that something about it fundamentally made no sense. It was patchy, like a strange elongation of a shadow, but there was nothing, really nothing, visible to me on either side of that road that could throw such a shadow.

It seemed to hover slightly above the surface of the road.

It glimmered in what evening sun was left.

This made me wonder if it was a pool of liquid of some sort, maybe a chemical spill, maybe deadly, so I slowed the bike and as I slowed I checked all round me for trouble. Then I brought the bike to a halt, parked it at the side of the road quite a distance back from whatever it was and stood and listened for anything unusual, all the time checking very carefully round me again just in case.

Then I set off towards the shadow.

What it was, when I got there, I could see clearly. It was a completely flattened person.

There was no face left on the head. There was nothing distinctive left of whoever this person had been, nothing but a gesture to the shape of something that had once been human. It was a skin from top to foot that had dried like leather, only marked by, I don't know what to call them, little borders, contours, in the places where some of the fabric that the person had been wearing had fused with what was now left of that person.

Dead on the road, I reckoned, and flattened by, well how could I know, a convoy of some sort, one of notable length and substantial weight that must've continued on this road for quite a time.

Maybe nobody had seen. Maybe they just didn't or couldn't stop to clear a stray cadaver off the road.

I mean, it's not that we weren't used to seeing the dead.

But this.

She shook her head.

Forgive me, girls.

Because, you see, I could've prised it off the road surface. Not easily perhaps, but I could have, I had a very good knife in my knapsack. I could've rolled that poor person up like a Turkish rug and carried it back to my bike under my arm, knotted it into the top of my knapsack, driven it away from there and seen to it that what was left of that person was given a decent burial. Or at least told somebody what I'd seen and where, so that they could do this instead.

I could have done many a thing.

But I didn't.

I didn't do a single one of the many things I could have done.

A lot of the things that have happened in my life have left me now, but not this. Time passing hasn't made it happen any less for me. I can still see it in front of me right now – exactly the same as we can see all these people dancing in front of us.

But rightly I shouldn't even have stopped the bike. Stopping for anything, stopping anywhere, was profoundly dangerous, not just to me but to countless others, and actually extremely stupid of me. It could very well have gone very wrong.

Do you see that? Do you?

She paused and I knew I was supposed to nod so I nodded at the lady who was now gripping my hand so tightly that the parts of my fingers I could see beyond her hand had gone quite white.

You understand, she said. This isn't something I've ever told a soul.

I nodded again like the very assiduous child I aspired to being.

Then I glanced past the lady to my little sister.

She was watching our mother dancing; the band's singer was now singing a fast song about seeing an alligator later and the people, including both our parents, were dancing much more energetically with their arms and legs flinging freely about and anyone who wasn't dancing was clapping along. My sister was clapping too. She had somehow managed at some point in the telling to detach her hand from the lady's hand. Or maybe the lady had voluntarily let go of her hand.

Instead what I did, the elderly lady said still holding my hand just as tightly, was this:

I got back on my machine. I started it up. I rolled it slowly forward and I steered it round the shape of the flattened person on the road without touching it.

Once I was past it I opened the throttle and carried on down that road to deliver what I'd been ordered to deliver, going at great speed between the mud banks, oh they were extraordinary, several feet high and red, clayey, with their tops curling back over themselves like waves in a sea that was parting to let me through.

Talk about the future is what it says at the top of the Duolingo unit I'm now on. It features a cartoon child with a cartoon frog on his head, a fishing net in his hands with which he's contemplating trying to catch the frog. The eyes of the cartoon child and the eyes of the cartoon frog are blinking and swivelling.

I am looking at this so as not to see the screen across the other side of the room where there's footage of a real child.

This child is very young, new in the world, only just kicking its legs, but at least it is, it's kicking them like anything though it's only weeks old and its legs and feet are nothing but skin on bone in a hospital bed in a hospital half in ruins in a city also in ruins.

The last time I looked directly at the screen this

child was looking, via whoever is holding the phone camera, straight back at me with wide open eyes.

The hospital the child is in is the only one left partially standing in a mostly flattened city across which dead people the colour of rubble are being dug out of rubble and shunted into bags then buried under rubble. An occasional live child the colour of rubble is pulled out of a building that's been turned into rubble and is carried as fast as possible in the arms of one of the still alive people who sift the rubble, who themselves resemble running pieces of rubble, towards the rubble that's the hospital.

I can't turn the TV news screen off. That would be an admittance not just of my hopelessness and helplessness but of my callousness. I leave it on because like everybody else now I'm a person who can cope with several screens.

So I'm sitting simultaneously clicking things on another screen which is sending sentence after sentence for me to translate from Italian into English or into Italian from English.

Actually this unit I'm on is titled wrongly. We're not just talking about the future here but about how to conjugate what I think used to be called – maybe still is called – future in the past:

> You can see it will not have been understood.
> It will have been used for something else.

Will they have remembered her?
They will have remembered something.
The door must not have been opened in a month.
Will the battery have died soon?
We will have called the doctor.
We will have watched the animals at the zoo.
I hope that by the time we arrive it will have
    been opened.
Won't he have expected a uniform?
She will have died for love.
He will have waited for this all week.
It must have followed me because it is hungry.

I've lost four out of five hearts and am about to be demoted to a lower league and don't have enough gems to see me through.

    Presto la batteria sara stata morta?

  I lose my last heart.
  I click off the language stuff.
  It is pathetic, pointless, reeks of irrelevance, I know, even to be thinking about old stories about those old wars that are so very over, whose dead, though they be piled on top of one another all round us across the world to the height and the breadth of a snowcapped piercing insurmountable mountain range stretching further than a human eye can see, are all so very, very, very gone. So much

so that they've become part of a landscape we don't even notice ourselves in any more, all the dead from the new wars spilling down the sides of it like avalanche.

But I've been thinking anyway about that thing I remember the elderly lady saying, about travelling on the motorcycle between the two sides of a hair parting as if crossing any surface could be like traversing the head of a giant living being, like the ground under our feet is part of a body so big that it can hardly be perceived by us tiny people crossing it.

I like that. Not unlike how I've enjoyed quite recently finding out that the human ear contains not just one but two labyrinths, and a vestibule, and windows, a round one and an oval one, and that there are canals, and things called temporal, and that there's wall, roof and flooring in the cochlear duct, and each ear has an aqueduct, and something that sounds like timpani, well, the drums of course, and there's something called the Organ of Corti – as if in every human ear there's not just the makings of every house and home plus some amazing natural and manmade architectural attractions any country'd be so proud of they'd be sending every tourist to see, but also the beginnings of the possibilities of an orchestra, or at least a small band.

The view inside a healthy ear through an

otoscope can resemble several things. A planet. A pearl. A sea creature. An ovum. An eye. The view inside an unhealthy ear can be shocking. A planet on fire. A planet like the one in the early silent film where the people get into a tin-can rocket, fly to the moon and hit the moon right in its eye, which drips down the moon's face as if the moon's made of a mix of pus and custard.

On the screen on the other side of the room, I can hear, the news item about the very small child and the methodical starving of a people has finished and now a politician is talking about how *our world* has *changed. Our world* is *now not the same as it has been.* Everything has *changed*, a *changed world order*; we now live on the *threshold* of a *new era* and the *old assumptions don't apply any more*; the *old assumptions have to go* now there's a *new world order* in our *completely new* world.

They've been saying this for some time. Because they keep repeating this it has started to sound rote, strangely mechanized, even quite panto-like as if asking for call and response *oh no it hasn't! oh yes it has!* or a bit like someone is shouting through a cartoon megaphone, telling us that the TVs and laptops and side desks and armchairs and radiators and wastebins and sofas and angle poise lamps, wallpaper, photos of loved ones in the picture frames, little containers with coffee in them or teabags still in date, even this chair I'm sitting in, are, whether we admit it or not, now the equivalent of the stuff that gets tucked behind thick red ropes hanging loosely between upright metal posts, cordoned off like rooms from the past in National Trust properties.

New era etc.

The reason they're saying it isn't to talk about how or why *our world* has changed. It's to justify massive expenditure on the weapons industry again to *keep us safe* in the *new era*, the doorway, or *threshold*, of which is already blocked up with the brand new dead.

I sit in the stupid museum of myself and act like it'll matter that I'm learning a language I don't speak from a machine.

I switch everything off.

There.

Silence.

Better.

Then birdsong from outside, the noise of traffic, the close-by rip-through of a moped: a food delivery, or one of the drug dealers arriving to do business in the playpark.

What can I do?

What could I ever do?

I phone my sister.

Hello stranger, she says.

Hi yourself, I say.

I'm amazed. You never phone me, she says.

Well, that's not strictly a true statement, is it, I say.

It was till you disproved it right now, she says. I'm honoured.

I say,

listen, what are those upright metal posts with the red ropes between them called again, like they have in galleries and museums and at those big publicity events where they have to keep the public back off the red carpets?

Hmm. I think what you mean is called stanchions, she says.

Stanchions. A word I've never used in my life, I say. So how come it still sounds like a word I know, like a word I'm familiar with, even though I don't and I'm not?

I mean, it means those rope posts in museums etc for crowd control, she says, but you might've come across it in a different context. It also has some nautical meanings and I think it has an architectural meaning. And if you ever worked on a farm I think they put cows in a stanchion to hold them steady for milking.

You know I've never worked on a farm, I say.

No, there've definitely been times in your life that have been quite mysterious to me, she says, and in one of those times you could quite easily have been working on a farm or doing something maritimey or architectural.

Do they really stand cows behind a museum cordon to get milked? I say.

No, it's like a kind of metal frame that you slip the cow's head and shoulders through then you tighten it to hold the cow in place. And it can mean temporary seating in a plane, and buses have them so people who are standing have something to hold on to –

Are you looking up the meanings of stanchion on your phone while we're talking? I say.

No, she says. I just happen to know what stanchions are.

But how? I say. How come?

Uh, she says. I've no idea. I just do.

Yeah, but how come you do and I don't?

Well, she says, I can't answer that, can I? And also. You could just have looked it up yourself, couldn't you? Instead of asking me. And then you'd have known.

Sure. I'd have known what it means for about five seconds, I say, the five seconds before I looked something else up and the word stanchion and its meanings faded away into the place in us where what we look up almost instantaneously goes to die. But now I'll never forget it. Because we've had this conversation about it.

Yeah you will, she says. £50 bet. I'll leave you a voicemail in a year's time. I'll say, what's a stanchion? And it'll be pointless because you'll probably not reply anyway. Do you even listen to your messages?

Ha ha, I say. Let's not go there.

Why do you need to know about stanchions anyway? she says.

I'm applying to do an evening class in museumry, I say. No, okay, I'm polyfilla-ing the holes in my vocabulary because I suspect that a great deal of what I know leaks straight out of me through those holes. Or a great deal of what the people who are changing the world and the era into something apparently completely changed and unprecedented and new where the old assumptions don't apply any more want me to think flows straight into me through those holes. Or both. What were you so busy doing that I interrupted?

She sighs.

Nothing. Actual nothing. Something equating to nothing. I was lying on my back on the living room floor staring at the ceiling berating myself about how I should be looking for a new job.

Yeah, you said in your note you lost your job, I say.

Yep, she says. For asinine reasons. Actually I must stop using that word, it's extremely unfair to donkeys which are very clever creatures and not at all foolish or stupid. Or maybe myself start using the word asinine to mean really clever and see if it catches on. What about you? What you up to?

Oh, the usual nothing, I say. Worrying about things I can't change. Glancing askance at my own life. In which what I've got left in my bank account is an amount more like the equivalent of that word change. Loose change.

I thought you were quite high up at Autonomy Clothing? she said.

Autonomy Clothing folded.

Ha ha! Sorry. Clothing. Folded. Sorry for laughing.

Yeah. Not funny at the time. I remortgaged the flat when they did. Now these walls I'm sitting between belong to a bank that also no longer has any branches I can go into if I were to want to ask some humans in person there about what to do when I run out of money.

At least you're working, she says. Weren't you doing some creative thinking thing at a college?

They shut it down too, even though it made money and had a huge intake with a very long waiting list. They said it was too creative. They got worried about student thought leading to overexcitement leading to irresponsibility leading to law suit. Now I work three days a week wearing a lanyard that says Assistant Audiologist.

A what? she says.

Ears, I say.

Where? she says.

On the side of your head, I say.

I believe you, even if I can't see them, she says.

One of the fundamental reasons that humans invented mirrors, I say. No, I do hearing tests for people in a cubbyhole at the hospital and write up the results so that whoever I'm testing can be passed on to a consultant for instant review. What I literally do is, I go and fetch whoever's coming to see the consultant from the waiting area. I introduce myself and sit them down next to the desk. I tell them I'm going to do a simple hearing test. I ask if they'll permit me to look in their ears with the otoscope. I give them the headphones. I give them the response button and tell them I'm going to want them to press the button every time they hear a sound. I adjust the headphones till they're the right size, I explain to them the headphones have to be very tight. I place the headphones on their ears and I sit down in front of my computer screen. I cue up the sounds. The computer records their responses on a series of graphs. I help them off with the headphones and I send them back to the waiting area and I send the results to the consultant. Then I go back to the waiting area for the next person.

Don't you have to be qualified to do that kind of thing?

I hope you're not suggesting that my excellent degree in archaeology and anthropology, for which I'll be paying off the loan for the rest of my life, isn't relevant qualification for the work I'm doing, I say.

Are you saying this in case I'm going to ask you to lend me money? she says.

Nope. If you ask me for money I'll always give you money. Even if I don't have it. Do you need money?

Always, thank you, but not from you, thank you. I'll sort it. I'm sorting it.

Are you? You sure? You okay?

I'm okay if you're okay, she says.

Uh oh, I say.

Now you're worrying about me, she says. Stop worrying. It does no earthly good. Go and do something. Go and relax. Go and, I don't know. Listen to some music. David Bowie. Stanchion to Stanchion.

Oh. No, I say. Don't start.

The Jam. Down in the Tube Stanchion at Midnight –

Stop now, I say, before it's too late.

– Don't Stanchion So Close to Me, that was the Police, and what about the Beatles And I Saw Her Stanchion There, and there's Tammy, Stanchion by Your Man, and Ben E King, Stanchion by Me, and who was it again who sang Stanchion in the Shadows of Love?

She sings the last three in her very tuneful voice. My sister has always had perfect pitch.

Pretty, I say. But I have to go now, probably to hospital, because your punning has made my ears bleed. As ever.

See? Some things will *never* change, she says. Talking of which. Did you read that book I sent you yet?

Yeah. It was okay, I say. It was quite good. I thought it was quite well written and everything. A bit too dark for me. A bit too clever-clever, a bit too on the nose politically, for a novel. I'd have preferred a bit more world building. And what's with all that horse stuff? It could've been a bit more sci-fi. But yeah, I mean thanks for sending it.

Thought you'd find it interesting, she says.

Yep, I say.

Can anything be too on the nose politically these days? she says.

You're interested in that stuff. I'm not. Never was. Plus ça change, I say.

I'll tell you what's changed. What's changed is, I don't know what to do with myself, she says. What can I do? What'll we do?

Phone a sister, I say. Talk about the many meanings of the word stanchion. Anyway. Apart from that. How you doing?

Oh, okay, she says. I'm still stanchion.

You're a survivor all right, I say. And how's the kid?

Fine. I think. Hard to know. Archly witty at the moment. Can't really be called a kid any more. She seems a lot more adult than I do to myself most of the time.

How's it with the birth mother?

Oh, okay at the moment, okay so far. Billie had a choice and elected to stay here. They see each other regularly, every month. It's worked out well, at least it's working well now, Kimberley's had help, is clean, has sorted her life out, is pregnant right now, Bill's looking forward to a small sibling. I mean it might go wrong at some point, but seems to me there's hope. Tentative steps.

Pass on my love.

I will, my sister says. Maybe come and see us

some time. We'd love that. Things okay with you both?

Oh, I say. God. There's no both. We're well over. We broke up about two years ago.

Ah, she says. I didn't know. Sorry. It's been that long since we.

Longer, I say. Don't be sorry. I'm all out of love and it's a total fucking relief. It's fine.

I'll ask that again, then, she says. Ready? Here goes. How's things with you?

Lovely, I say. Not a care in the world.

Years ago, a few days after that family party, us back home now in our own beds after the bed and breakfast bedroom with its tight tucked in cold sheets and the blankets that smelled of damp, I opened my eyes to a noise of something strange in the middle of the night.

What?

Loud breathing. My sister. I could tell from the sound that she was crying and trying not to make too obvious a noise.

I got out of bed and crossed the room, sat on the side of her bed in the dark.

Do you want me to go and get mum or dad? I said.

She made a noise that meant no.

Do you want me to do something that will help?

She made the no noise again.

I'm good at helping, I said. You know I am.

Nobody can help about this, she said.

I can, I said. Whatever it is. I can do something. What about if I went and got you a glass of water?

How will that help anything? she said.

It'll help you rehydrate, I said. It's very important to stay hydrated because it's important that you don't dehydrate.

She started to cry harder.

Do you want me to put the light on? I said.

Water or putting a light on won't help about this, she said.

Help about what? I said.

The dead flat person, she said.

Oh, I said. Are you still thinking about that?

She made a whimpering noise.

That was days ago, I said. Don't be scared about that.

Scared isn't what I am, she said.

She sat up in the bed, scrunched herself as far back against the headboard as she could get with her arms round her legs.

That story was just a story, I said.

It wasn't. It was true, she said. It happened. To that person the lady told us about.

But nothing like that's ever going to happen to you, I said.

You can't know that.

Yes I can.

You can't. Nobody can. And in any case I'm

not worried about it happening to me and I'm not scared. The thing I am is sore. I am sore like all through my whole body. It hurts from top to toe. It hurts like bloody billy-o. That's why I am doing this crying, not because I'm scared.

Do you remember when you had the mumps? What about if I go down and get you some disprin dissolved in water for the pain like I did when it got really sore then, remember?

She sniffed, wiped her nose against her pyjama sleeve.

Okay, she said.

I went as silent as possible downstairs without putting any of the lights on all the way to the kitchen. I didn't put the light on in the kitchen either. I filled the glass in the dark and fumbled about in the cupboard for the packet of junior painkillers. When I got back upstairs I put the water glass down on the carpet, closed our door over with care, held the handle tight in then let its little tongue back out into its slot in the doorframe millimetre by millimetre without making any sound. Careful in the dark I stepped wide over the place where I'd left the glass, I switched the bedside light on and I blocked the bottom of the door with one of the dressing gowns off the hooks on the back of it so if anyone woke up and saw the strip of light they'd not think it was us that woke them and be angry about it in the morning.

Here, I said.

Thanks.

She drank it.

Are you the kind of sore that someone needs to be told about so they can take you to a doctor? I said.

I don't think so, she said. I think it is the kind of sore that nobody medical can do anything about.

We sat for a bit until she stopped crying. Then we turned the volume to almost mute on the Game Boy and took turns on it for ten minutes.

Does it hurt less now? I said.

It still hurts across here where I breathe, she said. I think it is because of how there was nothing left of that person but an empty skin, and how sore it will have been to be made so flat, I mean back when it happened, because that soreness has been going round and round the world since, like a bird looking for somewhere to land, and it has landed on me.

Why has it landed on you?

I don't know. It just has. And Petra, what if nobody ever properly buried that person flattened on the road in the end and the person just got, like, thrown away, like in a litter bin or a skip or a landfill with people's rubbish all round the person?

The person won't have known much about it, I said.

She wrapped her arms tight around her own chest.

Also I don't know if they even had things like

litter bins and landfill back then, I said. I've never noticed any of those things in any old films from then or read about them in books about then or anything.

If they didn't have landfill, she said, where did they put their rubbish?

I think they had a lot less stuff to throw away in those days, I said. Anyway. What was left of whoever got flattened would've broken down naturally, being organic matter. Like the skin off an apple.

Organic matter, she said. Like an apple.

Then she looked down at her own arms. She took one of her feet in her hands and sat looking at her toes.

Matter doesn't matter, she said.

I saw she was about to cry again and that I'd have to be quick. So I lowered my eyelids sitting next to her on the bed, I put my hand to my ear as if I was holding a little earphone inside it like they did on TV in spy and aeroplane programmes or adverts on TV about people in call centres and I started making a very quiet humming sound like I was in a trance.

That worked. She looked up.

What are you making that noise for? she said.

Shh, I said, I'm just trying – oh. Oh. Hello. Yes. Hello. Thank you so much for answering my call. Yes. Yes, that's right. I'm calling because I hope you can help me, I'm trying to get in touch with someone we think might be there with you. No, I don't know a name yet.

Petra! my sister said. Don't!

I waved my hand at her to stop her speaking, like I couldn't hear properly when she spoke.

Yes, of course, I said into space. I'm Petra and I'm calling on behalf of my sister, her name's Patricia but we all call her Patch. Oh. Wild, we're the Wilds. Okay. So. So this is all we know. At the weekend we were away at this family sort of do and someone there told us something that happened to someone back in history and my sister was just wondering, we both were, we're both keen to know, how the person that it happened to is now. Yes, in spirit. That's exactly what I mean.

Petra, stop it. I'm not a baby, my sister said next to me.

I waved her away with a hand like our parents did when we tried to speak to them when they were on phonecalls.

Uh huh? I said. Okay. Well. I'm pretty sure it was in France, I think she said the south of it, and it was in the 1940s, near the end of the Second World War, and it was a person who was completely flattened on a road. But we don't know how. Maybe by something called a convoy. No. We don't know anything more than that.

I turned to my sister.

They've put me on hold.

Stop pretending, she said. You're not really speaking to anybody.

I'm speaking to a switchboard. They're playing, like, classical music while I'm waiting. Violins and stuff.

Why can't I hear it too then?

Well, you're maybe too young, it's maybe only for me to hear, or you'd literally be able to, like I am, you'd literally be listening to – oh.

I put my hand up like I was hearing a voice again, one that was difficult to hear.

Yes, I'm here, hello. Uh huh? Ah. Right. Yes, go ahead. Oh. Oh, hello. Hello. Oh my goodness. Yes. Yes. Oh, okay. Uh huh. No, that's amazing. That's so kind of you. Thank you so much for answering my call.

What? Who is it? What're they saying? she said.

Oh, I'm so glad. Thank you so much for telling us, I'll pass that on to her right away. I hope I didn't wake you or disturb your sleep or anything by us wanting to know. Yes. Goodbye sir, thank you so much and all our best wishes to you. Patch, quick, say goodbye. Say thank you.

Goodbye! my sister said looking into the space above my head. Thank you! And can I just ask this one –

I shook my head.

Gone, I said.

Where?

Back.

Back where? she said.

You know, I said. Gone like when someone hangs up the phone.

Who was it?

I don't know who I spoke to at first, but then it was him who came on the line.

Who?

The person. The person who got flattened.

The person! The person himself!

The switchboard fetched him. He told me I'm to tell you he's fine.

Did he say that? Really?

I nodded.

What else did he say to you? What did he say?

He said to tell you thank you.

He thanked *me*? she said. What for?

For thinking of him. And he says to tell you his painful days are over and they were over very quickly and though it *was* sad and it was definitely really excruciatingly painful when it happened back then, it didn't last long and it's been over for a very long time now and he doesn't want you to worry about him any more because that painfulness and that time are now completely gone.

Are they? she said. Really?

That's what he told me, I said. So it must be true. Coming from the horse's mouth and all.

He was on a *horse*? she said.

It's a saying. Horse's mouth. It means that what's being said is coming from the only place that can tell you something for real.

Why does it mean that?

Oh God I don't know. It just does.

From the only place that can tell you for real, she said.

I nodded.

She nodded back. Her mouth fell open.

Wow, she said.

I know, I said.

Did he say what it's like, the place he's in now?

No, not really, but I think it's okay, it sounded okay, I mean he sounded quite happy and everything.

What was his voice like?

It's a bit of a blur and honestly Patch it's already beginning to fade, I think that's because I'm obviously not meant to remember much about it for longer than the time it takes to tell you.

Tell me everything quick! Tell me what else he said before it fades!

Well. He definitely told me to tell you you've to slide yourself back down into the bed and not to worry about him ever again and that you've to close your eyes and go to sleep now because we've school tomorrow.

He knows we go to school? He knows about us? He knows about me?

Yep, and he said you've not to waste a moment of

your education and you've to work hard and learn and then teach people about how to, uh, make the world a much better and safer place than it was when he was, uh –

I was about to say killed but I stopped myself because I didn't want her to get upset again –

a boy, I said.

When he was a boy? she said. Did he say anything else about what it was like when he was a boy?

No, I said. At least, I don't think so. At that point it was getting quite hard to hear, like his voice was getting further and further away as he spoke. Like there was only this short time, this brief opportunity in which we'd be able to hear each other.

Oh, she said. Petra. You literally spoke to a dead person. It's amazing. What was his voice like?

It was like, uh, like lots of voices made into one voice, I said.

Like a choir? she said.

He also said I was to tell you we're both to go to sleep now and wake up tomorrow free from worry and that it's very, very important that you don't ever say anything about this conversation to mum or dad or anyone at school. Or anyone ever, actually.

Why not? she said.

He told me he's a very private person. He says they all are.

All who are?

It's to do with privacy. So I think it was very generous of him to grace us for a moment with his presence.

I had read the phrase about someone gracing someone else with presence for a moment in a book somewhere and knew it sounded right here. It worked, it was working. She was pushing back down into her bed again now.

So, are you feeling a lot less sore now? I said.

She nodded.

Will I put the light off? Will we go back to sleep?

Nod.

Light off.

I felt my way back over to my own bed and got into it. I closed my eyes.

Pause.

Petra, she said in the dark.

Uh huh? I said without opening my eyes.

What was it he said that made you say *oh my goodness* like that?

Uh. Oh yeah. He said. He said this nice thing. He said that he doesn't really like being reminded of what happened to him but that you thinking of him had made him very moved and pleased.

Oh.

Pause.

And Petra?

Mm hm?

When will you speak to him again?

Yeah, that's the other thing he said. He said that this was a one in a billion trillion experience and would never happen again and that it was only happening at all so that my little sister Patricia Margaret Wild of 59 Bear Crescent would be free of all that worry now and not have to feel pain on his behalf any more and that she never had to think of it or him or worry about any of it again.

He really said all that?

Yup.

He said my actual name?

Uh huh.

Did he say Patch or Patricia?

He was quite formal. He used your full name.

How did he know my middle name?

I'm really tired now. It was really quite tiring doing that long distance talking.

Yeah. Sorry. But Petra – there is this one other thing I really need to know.

I'm sleeping now. Good night.

I need to know if you found out did someone bury him in the end, I mean about where he ended up in the end?

I breathed like I was sleeping. After a few moments I heard her sigh out a high little sigh.

Soon I could tell from her breathing that she was asleep.

A couple of days after this I'd got home from school, I'd taken our mother her four o clock cup of tea and put it on her bedside table for when she woke up and now I was laying the table downstairs before our father got home with supper; it was fish and chip night.

I was playing the blades of two dinner knives off the sideboard trying out rhythms and pretending I was a world famous percussionist when the front doorbell went.

There was a small girl at the door. She was eight or nine years old. She was holding a photograph of a dog, a quite large Shetland collie it looked like, and she held it in front of her face outwards as if it was a votive offering.

Are you a friend of Patch's? I said.

Yes, she said.

Patch isn't home yet, I said. She'll be here in ten minutes.

I'm not calling for Patch, the girl said. I need you to talk to Shandy for me.

Is Shandy that dog? I said.

Yes, the girl said.

Is he lost?

She's a she, the girl said.

A tear came out of one of her eyes and ran down her cheek. She wiped it away with a furious hand and shook her head to stop herself. Her face became even more grim and determined.

Got put down, she said.

Ah.

I made a sign to the girl to wait a moment. I closed over the front door. I went to the foot of the stair and listened to make sure there was no sound of movement from my mother upstairs. I opened the front door again. The girl was still standing there exactly like before holding the photo of the dog out ahead of her.

Come in, I said.

I told the girl to sit on one of the kitchen stools. The stool was a high one and for a moment she didn't know how to get herself up on to it because it meant putting the photograph on the sideboard and she clearly didn't want to let go of the photograph. She tucked it under her neck into the collar of her dress and clambered up on to the stool. Then when she was settled on it she reached for the photograph and held it face out in front of her again.

How do you know my sister? I said.

We're in the same class.

Why do you want to talk to me?

She says that you can speak to people when they die or are dead, the girl said. I asked her could you speak to dogs that were too.

Did she tell just you or did she broadcast this information to lots of people?

I don't know, the girl said. I told her Shandy got put to sleep and she said she bet her sister could talk to a dog that'd been put to sleep.

What's your name? I said.

Conchine, the girl said.

What is it you want to know, Conchine? I said.

I want to know Shandy's okay and warm enough and that she has a basket there and that they are being kind to her, and I need to know that wherever she is they won't mind her chewing the edge of the basket. She always chews her baskets. Even the plastic ones.

I checked my watch.

Okay. We'll try, I said.

I brought my eyelids down low and started humming under my breath like I had the other night.

Is that you doing it now? the girl said.

I ignored her.

Hello? I said. Hello! It's me again. Petra. Petra Wild. Thank you for answering my call again. I have another request. Can I just check with you that Shandy the –

I opened my eyes. The small girl was watching me wide eyed.

What kind of dog is Shandy? I asked.

Collie cross, she said.

I turned my back to the girl and petitioned the striplight in our kitchen:

– just to check with you that Shandy the collie cross is okay. I'm asking on behalf of Conchine. And that Shandy is warm enough. Oh. Oh good. That's wonderful. And – what? Doing what? Thank you for telling me. I'll pass that straight on to Conchine. Thank you very much for your help. Goodbye.

I turned back to the small girl.

Not only is Shandy fine and warm and happy and not only has she already chewed through three baskets, I said, but you know what?

What? the small girl said through a brim of tears.

Shandy's a very determined dog, they told me.

The girl looked bewildered.

Did they? she said. I didn't know that.

So much so that she only sleeps when you're asleep. And Shandy has asked them to put her new basket quite close to your bed so she can keep an eye on you and listen out for you when you're asleep. You won't be able to see the basket, obviously, but it'll be there. And apparently they can't get Shandy to leave your side. In fact, we can't see her, but she's here right now.

Is she? the small girl said looking down at the floor. Where?

The main thing is, she's not in pain any more, I said. All the pain she had from being an elderly dog is completely gone now.

The girl shook her head.

No, that's wrong, she said. They didn't have her put to sleep because she was in pain or old. She was only six. They had her put to sleep because they're divorcing and my brother's going with my father and I'm staying with my mother and neither of them wanted to keep Shandy because my mother can't afford it and my father hates Shandy.

Yes, so, what I meant when I said not in pain any more was, I meant the pain of the divorce, all the pain of knowing, in that way that dogs know everything about us and that it was happening and it was painful and everything, I said.

No, you said she was old and she wasn't, the girl said.

Yes, but that level of pain, well, it was prematurely ageing your poor dog. Every day.

The girl looked at me. She looked doubtful.

Can *I* talk to Shandy just to be sure? she said.

Course you can. She's right next to you, I said.
Where exactly? the girl said.
My sister came into the kitchen.
Oh, hi Conch, she said.
Hi, the girl said.
Did she do it? my sister said to the girl, then turned to me and said, Conch's dog got put down. There was nothing wrong with it and they just put it down! It isn't fair.
She told me a minute ago that Shandy's right next to me, the girl said. I can't see where.
My sister glanced at the photograph in the girl's hands then squinted down at where the legs of the high stool met the floor.
I think I can see something, she said. Has your dog got, like, a front leg with white going up it like a white sock?
Yes! the girl holding the photograph said.
I can see something sort of glimmering, my sister said. There.
She pointed randomly at the floor near the stool.
Show your friend out for me now, please, Patch, I said. I've still to get things ready for supper.
The girl slid herself off the stool and went through to the hall with my sister. I heard my sister telling her to be careful not to shut her invisible dog in the door. When I heard the front door close and was sure the girl was gone I went into the hall too. I spoke quietly so as not to disturb our mother.

I told you not to tell anyone, I said.

My sister rolled her eyes.

I didn't tell anyone anything, she said.

You're a little liar, I said.

I didn't! I didn't say a word to a single soul. She just knew. She came up to me at school. She must just have known about you sidekickly, my sister said.

You mean psychically, I said.

I prefer the word sidekick to that word you just said, my sister said.

Yeah, but it's the wrong word, I said. You're saying the wrong word.

Yeah, and you never do anything wrong, my sister said. Or tell lies. Do you?

She gave me a mean look.

Then we both heard our father's car on the gravel in the drive.

Oh. Oh shit, I said.

To her credit she came through to the kitchen and helped me lay the table double quick so it was ready before he got himself out of the car and through the front door, and she managed to get most of the things she put on the table in their correct places.

About a week later a woman came to the front door when my sister and I were at school and our father was at work and rang the doorbell so insistently that our mother had to get up from her afternoon rest and come downstairs.

The woman told our mother that she'd heard she could contact the dead.

I can do what? our mother said.

We overheard our mother telling our father afterwards that when she heard the woman on the doorstep say this she'd laughed out loud like it was a great joke being played on her. But the woman had looked crushed and had insisted she'd heard on good authority that there was someone at this address who could do this and that she desperately needed to contact some dead people.

God, don't we all, our mother had said. There's

a few people up there or down there that I'd like to talk to too.

Our mother had invited the woman in and had made her a cup of tea.

I've a list of my dead's names here, the woman said and she handed our mother a piece of paper.

After she had assured the woman who took some persuading that there was nobody in our house who could do such a thing and after she'd got the woman out of the house, our mother had picked up the piece of paper which the woman had insisted on leaving just in case on the kitchen table.

She didn't know what to do with it. She couldn't bring herself to put it in the bin, a list of beloved dead people. She couldn't burn it. These things seemed disrespectful.

So she slipped some shoes on and took it down the street and over the main road to the supermarket where there was a recycling skip and she pushed it through the slot.

It had really tired her out to go and do this.

Then there was the different woman who started coming to the door. She came several times. Sometimes she came alone, sometimes she had an angry looking man with her and sometimes a baby buggy with a little dog strapped into it. All she would say was *I must speak urgently with the medium.*

Whenever we saw her coming I ran upstairs and hid in our bedroom.

She came three times over one weekend. Our father, who at first had seemed to find the situation quite funny, had to answer the door to her because our mother was now refusing altogether to get out of bed. His politeness ran out the fourth time he opened the door and saw that this woman was holding out a wedge of banknotes. He knocked them out of her hands and they blew all over the front garden. My sister and I watched from an upstairs window as the woman and the man went round the lawn picking them up.

Then we were eating breakfast the Monday or Tuesday after and we could see through the kitchen window that our father was speaking to someone standing in the lane over the back fence. When he came in he told us that the man he'd been speaking to was the father of the girl called Conchine.

He'd come round to ours to complain because his daughter had taken to dragging the dead dog's lead around after her with its empty collar attached, and that after she'd been given a stern telling off for doing this she'd run away from home with another schoolfriend. They'd been missing for two days. There had been a full on police search and both girls had been brought home in a police car after they were spotted in a public park in a town a couple of railway stops away, and now his wife was blaming him for the dog being put down and the distress of her child, and would be using all of this as a negotiating tactic in their divorce proceedings.

I hope Conchine was in the dog-friendly part of that park when they found her, my sister said and we both burst out laughing.

But our father went pale. Then he went a dark red colour. He slammed his fists on the kitchen table so hard that everything on it shook then he lifted me out of my seat from behind by the scruff of my school shirt and pullover, turned me still hanging in the air round to face him, held me level with his head at arm's length and shouted at me while he shook me like a dog shakes a rabbit.

When I began to choke he dropped me back on to the lino.

Here are some of the things he shouted at me that morning:

> little histrionic hysterical
> playing your stupid bloody games
> my reputation
> troublemaking beyond belief
> you little fool
> neighbours laughing
> me a laughing stock
> as if I haven't enough to worry about
> no wonder your mother is like she
> shame and ridicule on our house and home

ashamed of you
silly little bitch

After that I had to go upstairs and change my school shirt because the collar had ripped away on one side from the body of the shirt. I did this quite solemnly, in what felt like a blest and special state of shock, as if I were going through some kind of rite ceremoniously unbuttoning one shirt and taking it off then putting my arms into the sleeves of and buttoning the other, to the sound of both our father and our mother shouting downstairs at the tops of their voices, my mother angry because he'd used language that she didn't want him to use to refer to us, all through which argument he repeatedly used the kind of language she said she didn't want him to use, which only made her even angrier.

After that morning it all quietened down a bit.

Nobody else came to the door, at least not that we knew about or got told about.

Handwritten letters from people we didn't know did keep coming through the letterbox for another few weeks. For a while the phone rang a lot, often at late hours of the night or early hours of the morning. Partly it was drunk people laughing. Partly it was drunk people crying.

Our father bought an answerphone and turned the phone ringtone wheel to silent.

I remember now – I hadn't remembered till

thinking about it now just opened it in me all over again, like a book – that when I got home after school on that same day of him shaking me in the air, and came upstairs with her four o clock cup of tea, our mother was awake.

Not just awake. She was sitting up waiting for me.

She patted the side of her bed. I sat where she patted. She took one of my hands in both of her hands.

You know that living people really shouldn't, really mustn't, mess with the dark things you're messing with, Petra, don't you? she said.

I wasn't messing with anything, I said. I didn't. I wasn't.

You know it's very powerful and very dangerous to go near these things and that anyone who does might very easily be driven mad? she said.

I was just pretending, I said. Honest. It wasn't real. It was made up.

I don't want to live to see any daughter of mine be driven mad, she said.

I was just going to do it the once, I said. The second time wasn't meant to happen. It just did.

There are some things it doesn't do to think about, she said. There are some things you can't preoccupy yourself with. You can't waste your time thinking about those things. You can't do anything about them. You just have to accept them. Do you understand?

I nodded.

Not that I'm not proud of you for trying. Myself I think it's quite admirable. Your father doesn't understand. He's scared by it. Your sister won't understand. She has a thinner skin than you do. You're as tough as good boot leather. So I do understand. But I'm telling you straight. I hope you can hear me when I tell you. There are things in life we have to know to leave alone.

I didn't mean any harm, I said. I was just trying to make people feel better, I just pretended it one night to make Patch stop crying when she was upset about something. I know that the ghosts, and the dead people and all that, I know they don't exist. It was just a, a –

I see, she said. A jeu d'esprit.

A what? I said.

For kindness' sake. But just in case you were even half serious. You'll not do it again. You'll stop it now. That's it over now. You understand?

Yes, I said.

All well and good, she said. Now.

She kissed me on the side of the head. Her breath smelled of warm bed and of her.

Go and lay the table so it's done and ready before he gets home, she said.

Okay, I said.

I did. I put the knives and forks out one by one, moving with care in the different air of my mother's forgiveness. Contrite, simultaneously told off and understood – more, metaphysically admired and permitted – I grated the extra cheese into a bowl and watched it come apart from its block with something like a heightened understanding of what it might mean to be both whole and shredded.

    I was getting the frozen pizzas out of the big freezer in the garage when my sister came in and stood behind me.

    She held something out towards me. I took it.
    It was a twenty pound note.
    What's this for? I said.
    I found it in the front garden on Sunday, she said. I saw it in the flowerbed, it got caught round the roots of one of mum's rose bushes.
    That's okay. You found it. You keep it, I said.
    I held it back out. She shook her head. She told me she had been going to keep it for herself, had decided to do that and tell nobody about it, but that someone – she said a name I couldn't make out – thought that rightly it was my money, I'd been the one that earned it and I should have it.
    Who? I said.
    [ ], she said.
    What she'd said sounded like the word glyph.
    Glyph? I said.
    Yes, she said.
    Like, egyptian? Like hieroglyph?
    Sort of. But that's not why he's called it.
    Who on earth's Glyph? I said.

Jeu d'esprit.

Spirit game, literally.

Less literally: witty mind game. Ingenious or childlike thinking exercise. Light hearted display of wit or cleverness.

I'll have looked it up, back then I mean. I'd have done that in a dictionary though, rather than online. There still weren't that many computers in 1996. We didn't have one till later.

I looked it up again right now a few minutes ago, on one of my screens.

Of course, our mother died soon after the time I'm remembering. Our mother was thirty eight years old.

It wasn't violent death. It was a quiet, sad death, of course a young death relatively,
I mean compared to all the people who live

longer, and to other people my age's mothers' deaths.

Of course, our father died too, twenty two years later, eight years ago now.

Of course we argued over selling the house and who got what and who did what.

Of course we went our separate ways after a great deal of animosity about each other's irresponsibility, Patricia and I.

She works in tech stuff now, well, she did; up until recently she was apparently employed at a massive PR agency as a spotter of AI text in the online presences of a full portfolio of businesses whose publicity outputs the agency looks after. Her job was to rewrite it where she found it to make it sound more human so it would appeal more to the people who read it. When she sent me the parcel a couple of weeks ago, the note she enclosed told me this, and that she'd just been made redundant and replaced by a digital assistant because artificial intelligence is now thought to be better than any human not just at spotting artificial intelligence in advertising copy but also at rewriting it to make it sound more human.

She'd sent me that book, too, a contemporary novel. Dystopia. Neither being the kind of thing I like to read.

The note to me she tucked inside the book said: *saw Billie was reading this – a book! rather* *than Busjam or killing something on a screen or probably god forbid but what can I do about it f*ck all whatever self hurt or porn or bullying they're sending round each others phones – phone usually glued to the hand but for three whole days it was nothing but a book – couldn't believe my eyes when I saw its title Gliff – thought of us then – also not just the title made me think of us – I bought one for me and sneak-read it to check on the quiet it was okay for Bill to be reading & thought its rather good about siblings so here it is – for you from yours truly – me xx*

How did my sister ever get a job writing or checking copy for anybody when her basic syntax is such a car crash?

Maybe doing that work is what's made her syntax a car crash.

But yes, it *was* good about siblings. Also, since I read that book, in fact I think because I did, I have now remembered several things I'd flat out forgotten.

I'd forgotten the story about the man who was something to do with our great grandfather, the man they shot in the First World War for helping a horse.

I've never forgotten our father shaking me – I still hold it against him, among other things, even though he's been dead nearly a decade – but I'd totally blocked why he did it.

I'd forgotten the family party, the model village. Our mother dancing to the fast song about the alligator like light and happiness were coming off her in waves.

The whole jeu d'esprit conversation.

People coming to the house looking for solace.

That poor small girl whose dog they put down.

Glyph.

I'd completely forgotten Glyph.

Where's this 'Glyph' then?

We were in our bedroom. We were speaking in low voices. We had twenty minutes at the most before our father'd be home and I had about half that time before I'd have to put the grill on, take the pizzas out of the oven, add the extra things to them and put them under the grill.

Oh, he's not here *now*. He *was* here, before, she said. He was sitting there.

On *my bed*?

Yes.

Where's he now? I said.

How would I know?

Well, how did you get him to come here?

I didn't. He came by himself. He was just right there, then he stood up and stood by the window. I've seen him a few times today. He was here this morning after dad shouted at you too.

What, in here? Watching me change my shirt?

No. I mean downstairs, she said. After you were getting shouted at. I think he always stands by a curtain. So he can hide behind it if he needs to.

Yeah. Sure he does.

He *does.*

Did mum and dad see him?

No.

Did you?

She nodded.

He's not invisible then?

Not to me, she said.

What's he look like? Is he, like, a Halloween skellington?

I said the word like this because Patch was so frightened of skeletons she was even capable of freaking out when she heard the word skeleton.

No! she said.

So you're not scared?

Nope, she said. He's not scary. He's nice.

Is he two dimensional? I said. I mean when he turns sideways does he look a bit flattened?

She thought about it. She shook her head.

Could you roll him up like a poster or a rug? I said.

No, she said. He's just like us. Really like *we* are.

The same. Except he's quite blurred. And he's thin, she said. And he's sort of proper looking.

What's that mean?

He looks like that actor mum likes.

Which actor?

The one in the black and white film about Greece, she said. The one that sounds like it's going to be about someone ill on the moon.

Which?

Where they kidnap the German in the car and take him into the mountains.

Ill Met by Moonlight? He looks like Dirk Bogarde?

He looks like the one in charge. The thin faced one.

Yeah, Dirk Bogarde, I said.

I don't know. Whatever, she said.

With the moustache? I said.

I don't think he's got a moustache. It's quite hard to see. He sort of has blurry light round him.

What's he wearing?

He's dressed like the man you said the name of in the film.

Like a Greek person, with the hat with the little tassels? I said.

No, not when he's pretending to be a Greek person. Like when he's a *soldier*.

Wearing what?

Uh. I don't know. A shirt?

You're so making this up.

I am not.

You're a little squit, I said.

I don't care if you believe me or not, she said. I don't need you to believe me. I know I saw him and I know he was here. I know I spoke to him and he answered.

It's not someone who's somehow got into the house off the street and is hanging around in our bedroom? I said. Like a homeless person?

I bent down to look under the beds. Nothing, just the suitcases, the shoes. I went over to the window and punched the curtain on one side. Then I punched the curtain on the other side. Nothing. Just the venetian blinds rattling.

Listen, she said while I did these things. It's *him*. The man the lady told us about. The man you spoke to the other night to see if he was okay.

You do know, Patch, that I was just pretending to speak to someone that night when you were upset? I said. You aren't stupid enough to think that was all real? You do know it was all made up and I was pretending I was having a conversation? I didn't really hear or speak to anybody. I was just trying to make you feel better. You do realize that there wasn't really anybody there answering me?

Well, she said. Whoever you thought you weren't speaking to must've heard you after all.

What has whoever this is that *you're* speaking to said to you? I said.

He doesn't say much. When he does he just says this same word over and over. Every time, she said.

She made a noise that sounded partly like a cough, partly like someone breathing out very suddenly.

Glllf, she said. I said to him, is that what you're called? and he said it again. *Glllf. Glllf*.

How do you know that's his name? I said.

I don't, not for sure, she said.

Are you calling him that because of the egyptian thing because you're thinking of someone flat like an egyptian sideways person in a historical frieze? I said.

No, she said. It's because it's the only word he says. I think it's all he *can* say.

How many times have you heard him say it?

I don't know. Eleven times? Twelve?

And he hasn't said anything else?

Not that I've heard, she said.

So if that word's all he can say how do you know he thought I should have the twenty pound note? I said.

I felt it, she said. He made me feel it so I heard the words in my head. In a kind of voice that sounded like more than one person speaking at once.

Now I know you're lying. You're just copying what I made up and told you back on that first night, I said.

I'm not, she said. You can make stuff up if you like. I'm not making anything up. I heard it. In my head. And also, when I heard what he meant and he knew I had, he smiled at me and he nodded his head like this, yes.

How do you know it's *him*? I said. How can you be sure it's not just someone else who's dead? It could be *any* old person.

I just know. And he's not old, she said. I mean, he's older than us. I mean he's definitely an adult person. But a not very old one. He's way younger than mum or dad.

Okay, enough of this. If he exists. Make him come now so I can go and do the pizzas, I said. Where is he?

We stood. We waited. Nothing happened.

I shrugged my shoulders and made a disgruntled sound. I wandered across the room and picked a piece of paper up off the desk in the corner where we did our homework. It was a page torn out of a school jotter. Both sides were covered in my sister's handwriting; she had clearly been practising signing her name in many different ways. Some were florid. Some were dashed off like she was a tennis player signing a ball with a squiggle at Wimbledon. Some were done with care. Some looked like she was determined to fake her own name. PW PW PMW PMW PMW Patricia Wild Patricia Wild Patricia Wild Patch Wild Patch Wild Patch Patch Patch

Patch Patch (with an underline curving round under the name) Patch M Wild (with the underline coming off the end of the d at the end of Wild and going down the page over the signatures below it in a descending swirl like an Elizabethan death warrant) Patricia Margaret Wild Patricia Margaret Wild P. Margaret Wild P.M. Wild PM Wild Patricia M. Wild Patricia M Wild.

Which one of these signatures is you? I said.

All of them, she said.

I had two minutes before I had to get downstairs to stop the pizzas drying out. I waved the piece of paper in the air.

How about, what about, if you wrote down his name? I said. Maybe that would be a bit like. You know. Summoning him.

Okay, she said.

She came over to the desk and sat down, tore a fresh page out of a school jotter.

How do you spell Glyph? she said.

She wrote it down. She wrote it down again. She wrote it again all along the line at the top of the page.

Glyph Glyph Glyph Glyph Glyph Glyph Glyph Glyph

What if this Glyph person means you harm? I said. What if he means us all harm? What if you're messing with something that brings harm on us all and it's something that people shouldn't mess with or they go mad?

He doesn't mean anyone any harm, she said. He's here to tell us *about* harm, not to *cause* harm.

How do you know that? I said.

She turned back to the desk.

I just do, she said. It's not my problem if you don't.

Couldn't you hang out with the ghost of Shandy instead? I said. It'd be a lot simpler.

Shandy belongs to someone else, she said.

Glyph doesn't belong to you, I said.

Glyph chose me, she said. He's my friend.

He's not your friend, I said.

You mean, he's not *your* friend, she said. You're just jealous of him being in contact with me and not you.

You're being histrionic and hysterical.

You are, she said.

Stupid game, I said.

I'm not playing a game, she said.

I left her in the room by herself and went downstairs to do what I was meant to be doing.

I miss seeing people's handwriting these days.
   I miss my own. I write things by hand so rarely now that my own writing's become so unused to me and me to it that I myself can hardly read it.
   Back when we were clearing our father's house I found an old lined notebook in the odds and ends kitchen drawer. I opened it. It said on the top line in my child-handwriting the words

   Big Business   The Living Ghost   Wrong Again

and underneath, in my sister's even younger child-handwriting, these words copied down over and over again.
   For a minute I couldn't think why I would ever have written these things or she would've wanted to copy them.

Then I remembered:

the sharp faced girl at school in the year below me and the year above my sister, who lived up the road from us and who was exceptionally good at subtly bullying people, especially my sister.

One day, the summer before my sister started school, this girl who lived up the road was playing in our garden with my sister and I heard her telling Patch that school was terrifying, that learning to write was the hardest thing you'd ever have to do, and that being made to write whole sentences was like torture and you got into real trouble at school if you couldn't do it.

My sister, aged five: tears dropping into the stew on her plate at the kitchen table.

Don't cry, our mother said. Petra will show you what to do and help you practise. She's very good at handwriting.

So I'd sat with Patch at the table several August days in a row.

I wrote all the letters, capital and small, in a notebook, leaving the lines free below for her to use.

When she could do the letters, I wrote some sentences.

I don't want to do whole sentences, she said. They are like torture.

Okay. How do you feel about phrases? I said.

I don't know, she said. What *is* a phrase?

I realized I didn't know how to describe a phrase.

A phrase is a thin bit of a sentence, I said. If you imagine that the whole sentence is Oliver Hardy, then a phrase is more like Stan Laurel.

I said this because that was the summer my sister and mother loved watching Laurel and Hardy films. I loved them too. Our mother kept somehow getting hold of their films on video, I don't know where from, and slotting them into the mouth of the machine on the rainier afternoons before our father came home all that long summer.

There was one particular film that my sister thought so hilariously funny and laughed so much at that she fell off the couch on to a rug on the floor then rolled about on the rug, rolling it round herself like a cocoon and laughing like anything inside it. She laughed so much that all three of us ended up crying with laughing in a heap on the floor.

On the first page of that notebook

Big Business   The Living Ghost   Wrong Again

in both our handwritings. On the next few pages alphabets, higher and lower case. After that a page with a single sentence in my handwriting at the top:

The horse is white.

Underneath, all down the page, there were her handwritten copyings of this sentence.

I flicked through the notebook and saw I'd written a sentence on the top line of each page:

The horse is white.
The horse is called Blue Boy.
The horse is inside a house.
Horses aren't allowed inside houses.
The rich man owns the house.
He thought they were bringing him his painting.
His painting is called Blue Boy too.
The horse and a painting have the same name.
But they brought the horse instead.
The rich man is upstairs.
He does not see the horse come into the house.
He shouts down to Stan and Ollie.
Put Blue Boy on the piano.
They get the horse up on to the piano.
The horse is standing on top of the piano.
It is a grand piano.
The horse keeps knocking Stan's hat squint with its nose.
Stan thinks it is Ollie who is knocking his hat.
Ollie goes underneath the piano to get something.
A piano leg breaks.
Ollie gets squashed by a grand piano.
But also by the horse that is still standing on the piano.

I could see now that Patch had clearly had trouble with the word painting and the words squint and squashed.

When I'd found and read that notebook in our father's house I'd thought of that film and us all laughing, and I'd laughed. But right then Patch was in the other room bagging up our father's clothes. At this point, even though we were in the same house, we were relentlessly not speaking to each other.

I stopped laughing. I put the notebook in my bag. I didn't show her it.

I still have that notebook.

It's in a drawer in the bedroom.

At least I didn't throw it out.

If I were to compare it to the handwritten note she sent with that book last week I would probably actually still be able to see her child self in its thirty-years-later curvature.

All of us, in a heap, laughing our heads off.

Our mother: her head above the bedclothes like she might only be a head, there might be no continuation of a body below, and the way I'd dare myself silently closer and closer to check that the bedclothes were moving so I'd know she was definitely still there, still breathing, still alive. I can see the little flowerheads on the pattern on the long gone duvet cover bend away from me and towards me again as she breathes and the slight shift in them is relief.

Our father: the flare-up of him as fast as a struck match.

But he was urbane too, making any neighbours disputing anything with him relax and laugh along with his bonhomie; pulling our car in to the side of the road suddenly to offer someone a lift if he saw someone he knew walking along the road towards town.

There he is, out one late summer evening in the driveway, he's painting the fence along the side of the house with creosote so it will last the winter and he's whistling. I can quite literally smell the creosote. I can quite literally hear the tune.

Old song. Me and My Shadow.

Actually Glyph's here right now, my sister said.

Where? I said.

You don't know, she said. Because you can't see him, can you? Only *I* can see him.

It was a quite cold Sunday afternoon round about Eastertime. We were over by the riverside; it was one of the days when our mother couldn't get up at all and our father had got us out of the house by giving us money to go and play crazy golf at the place that had reopened after the winter, and we'd dutifully done that, hitting the balls at the fun constructs. Now we were kicking stones around before dusk in the weird space in the park that had once been a sort of open sided pavilion and these days was just a platform, like a stage with a wide square of concrete stretching away from it that in our mother's day had been used for roller rinking and open air dancing and was now heavily cracked and scattered with twigs and crisp bags, broken glass, finished bits of cigarette, beer cans in the old leaf litter.

There were a few people still wandering about on the park paths and some other kids we didn't know calling to each other across the pavilion space.

There was a man over there pushing a pram through the trees.

I can, I said. That's him over there.

No it isn't. Anyway he's gone again, she said. But he was at the Crayzee Course. Did you see him *there*?

I saw something, I said. I think he was there at the helter skelter hole and the lighthouse hole.

She shook her head.

I was just testing you. He wasn't ever at the Crayzee Course.

Maybe you just didn't catch sight of him there yourself, I said. You don't even know what his name means.

I do, she said. I do know.

I looked it up, I said. It means something carved or engraved into something else. Something that makes an impression in it. Like making a mark not just on a surface but in a surface. It also means something that means because it's a symbol.

No it doesn't, she said. You can say what you like. I know what it means. It means the noise he makes when he breathes out.

She did the L for loser shape with her fingers on her forehead.

You may as well admit it, she said. You don't really know him. He's only visible to me.

I admit I do find it quite hard to see him, I said. But I can hear him really clearly.

You can *not*, she said. And you told me you just made that hearing thing up.

You don't know what I can hear and I can't, I said. Only I know that.

Did you hear him last night when we were supposed to be asleep? she said.

How could I? I said. I was asleep.

He was telling me about what his life was like when he was a boy, she said.

How? I said. You said he could only say the one word glyph over and over.

I told you. He tells me inside my head without words. Then it becomes words.

Okay, so. What was his life like when he was a boy?

Maybe you have to wait until he tells *you*. Maybe only *I'm* supposed to know, she said.

Nobody's told you anything, I said. You don't know the first thing about him being a boy.

I do. He's told me loads.

Like what? Just tell me one thing he told you.

Well. He said. Uh. He said he was one of seven children and their father was a captain and they didn't have a mother.

Uh huh? And what else?

He said they had a governess instead and she was a good singer and they used to play tricks on her, and one of them put a big pine cone on her seat for a practical joke and she sat on it and jumped in the air but then she didn't dob any of them in to their father for doing it so they knew she was a good sort.

Mm hm, I said. Keep going.

I don't think I should tell you any more facts from a private conversation between him and me, she said.

Just one or two more things, I said. Just so I can get the picture.

He said they hid with his family in a graveyard when the soldiers were looking for them. Then he escaped over a mountain, they all did. The mountains were really beautiful. But in the end he got caught and they put him in a place called the hole in a prison camp. It was really dark in there. But he escaped when he stole a motorcycle and jumped over a prison fence on it.

She checked my face to see whether I'd spotted that for details she could use she was raiding all the films she'd seen that she could remember having something about wars in them.

Is that everything he told you? I said.

No, that's just some of what he told me, she said. There's loads more.

She looked small; she looked chilled. The light was waning. It was definitely colder now. I took my jacket off. I sat closer to her and put the jacket round both our shoulders so we were both inside the one jacket.

He told *me* some things too, I said.

You can't see him, she said.

But I can hear him.

You're just faking, she said.

I was at first. This time I'm not faking.

When did he tell you? she said.

When you were asleep.

No he didn't, she said.

I sighed.

Okay, I said. Whatever.

I kicked my heels in my boots against the concrete base of the stage. She started doing it too. First we kicked out of time with each other. Then we were kicking in perfect time. When I stopped kicking she did too.

What kind of things did he maybe tell you if he maybe told you anything? she said.

Oh, about what it was like when he was a boy and so on, I said.

Like what?

He told me he had an older sister. But she died young.

Did he? Why did she die?

She coughed up blood one day, I said. Her name

was Mary but everyone called her Minnie. Min. She was born five years before he was. She died when she was sixteen and he was the same age as I am now. She was clever. She went to a grammar school. She taught him to read when he was still too small for school and their parents were astounded when one day he wrote his name on the wall in their house. They were angry too because he wrote it with a bit of fishing rod with a sharp end, and they had just put up expensive new wallpaper with roses and rosebuds on it, and he wrote it really big by pressing the end of the fishing rod through the new paper and tearing it all up the wall. And his sister, she really liked books. She was always borrowing books from a library in a chemist's shop.

Chemists don't have libraries in them, my sister said. Like she went to Boots the chemist and there was a *library* in there! I don't think so.

I felt myself blush. It did sound stupid. I hated getting things wrong. I didn't know why I'd said that stuff about a library in a chemist's; it had come into my head from nowhere.

I'm just telling you what he told me, I said.

Like a library's going to help make people not ill! Like a library is anything to do with health! she said.

He told me that's how she taught him to read, I said. From words she showed him in books from the library. She would point to the word and ask him what it said. He told me he remembers she brought home a book called The Dream and that's the book where she showed him that when the word *flow* was part of the word *flowers* it had to be said differently. Unless you were talking about something flowing.

And anyway, my sister said, that's not really facts about *him*. That's more like a lot of facts about *her*. Or about *words*. You're just trying to distract me from everything you're saying being rubbish by saying stuff about other people and words.

I stopped saying anything. So did she.

The evening was coming down. The park, open till dusk, was emptying. I didn't want us to get locked in.

I took the jacket off us both and slipped it back on. I jumped down off the ruined stage. So did she, though it was quite a far jump for her; my sister was still small.

She looked up at me, stolid, pale with cold. I gave her my scarf. She wound it round her neck under her chin and I tucked its long ends into her buttoned up coat so they wouldn't drag on the ground. We took the path home that went past the cemetery.

I couldn't have known, when I was a child, or if I did I couldn't ever have articulated, the modicum of guilt and responsibility that there is in making someone real up.

Now I sense it sharply, the wrongness in what we were doing, using a terrible true story, the ghost or the shade of a story, about something abysmal that I'm assuming really did happen to someone real, to distract ourselves from feeling what we must no doubt have been feeling, and sensing, round what turned out to be – and look at me now even in this sentence still keeping it at a distance – our mother's impending death.

So tonight, after speaking to my sister on the phone, I decide to spend time looking up things online that might help me source something, anything, real and true about the flattened person that the elderly lady told us about thirty years ago.

Right.

First I try to look the elderly lady herself up to see if by some miracle she's still alive, which I doubt because I remember her as strikingly old, or if there's anyone I can find to contact to ask about her and about the story she told us.

Someone somewhere, possibly more than one person because there were a few camera flashes happening round us when we were placed sitting next to her, will have a copy of that photograph that got taken of us.

We never had much contact with extended family. None at all with our father's family. Our mother's parents both died young and I know it was a sadness to her that she no longer spoke to her brother, our uncle, because of animosity between him and our father. The only time we saw our uncle was after she died; a slight shy much older man, he came to the house after the funeral and he'd brought us presents, Talking Teletubbies, which even my sister was by then far too old for.

Our father rigorously avoided his own family.

I never knew why.

I realize now how unusual it was, and how surprising, that we ever attended *any* family party.

But someone somewhere one day invited the elderly lady to a party at the same time as they invited our parents, and if she was family then someone in his family might know.

But I have literally no way of contacting anyone in his family.

The computers in our house that will have had anything family based or useful in any email inbox were cleared of their history caches and donated away eight years ago.

Anyway it was way too early for that invite to have been virtual. It'll have come through the post or over the phone.

The address book in which our mother kept anything about both sides of the family, God knows where that went. It will have disappeared into what became the junk pile up of our father's house and probably we threw it out in the clearing.

I type into the search bar *silver wedding party 1996 bourton-on-the-water.*

Listings for places where you can hold silver wedding celebrations in Bourton-on-the-Water come up.

I look up *bourton-on-the-water hotel silver wedding party March 1996.*

Nothing of any use comes up.

I go back to the first page of links and look up some hotel sites in Bourton-on-the-Water to see if I recognize anywhere.

I try looking up pictures of Bourton-on-the-Water bed and breakfasts.

Edie.

She said that her name was Edie.

I look up *Edie intelligence ww2*.

The net comes up with a lot of links to a spy, a double agent called Eddie Chapman.

I try again using all the surnames I can remember hearing being connected to our father. I'm not even sure that I'm not now making those up.

Edie Wild. Edie Martin. Edie Shaw.

It comes up with someone at Bletchley called Eddie Shaw who did transcript translations.

I try these combinations again using the name Edith. Then Edwina.

The net gives me many links to Edith Cavell and a sole link to someone called Edith Kup, a plotter and intelligence officer in the WAAF. I bookmark an interview with her on the Imperial War Museum site to listen to later.

I look up ancestry.co.uk.

The net gives me eight thousand Edie Wilds and six thousand Edith Wilds, eighty eight thousand Edie Martins and seventy three thousand Edith Martins, then twenty six thousand Edie Shaws and twenty two thousand Edith Shaws.

Six thousand Edwina Wilds, seventy four thousand Edwina Martins and twenty two thousand Edwina Shaws.

It asks me to subscribe to look anything up about any of them.

Maybe there's an easier way to go about this. Maybe someone somewhere has written a book about the story she told us. Ideally, rather than *her* name, I'd like to find a name for the person, whoever they were.

I try looking up *book about flattened person south of France near end ww2*.

The net sends me to an encyclopedia entry about an 1884 book by someone called Edwin Abbott Abbott about a land called Flatland where the people are all two dimensional and seem to be named after geometric shapes.

I try looking up newspaper reports about a body found flattened on a road in the south of France in 1945.

Lots of links about many atrocities come up.

None of them as far as I can see features a flattened person.

I look up *flattened body on road france ww2*. I am presuming there must have been at least a few flattened people.

The net gives me a thread on Reddit about the Brad Pitt 2014 film called Fury, which apparently features a flattened person. One of its correspondents says this scene originates in a French book called Le chemin le plus long, published in 1997 and featuring eye witness stories told by Free French veterans, where in one statement a tank regiment and several days' worth of other vehicles really do flatten a person's corpse.

But that's in Bavaria, not France.

Someone else further down the thread notes that there's a similar image in the film Cross of Iron; someone else declares themself *a steamroller baby, rolling down the line, so you better get out of my way now, before I roll all over you,* which I discover when I look it up is a US military cadence or call and response song. Someone else suggests the flattened person image also turns up in the most recent film version of All Quiet on the Western Front, which won many awards. The net also unearths an autobiographical Italian book called La pelle, from 1949, in which someone apparently picks up the skin of a flattened person off a road and waves it in the air like a flag.

But I can't, in an initial attempt anyway, find anything out about anything I remember of the story we were told.

In any case, when I think of that person, I can't not think of the fictional version I made up for my sister.

Way more clear than any flattened self, vivid in my head there's a small boy perched on the arm of an armchair in which his own sister is sitting.

She's pointing to a word in a book. The word is flowers. The book is called The Dream.

Hmm.

I type into the search bar the words *book called The Dream* followed by *1920s*. I reckon that's the right decade for them.

Wikipedia. The Dream (novel).

The Dream *is a 1924 novel by H. G. Wells about a man from a Utopian future who dreams the entire life of an Englishman from the Victorian and Edwardian eras, Harry Mortimer Smith. As in other novels of this period, in* The Dream *Wells represents the present as an 'Age of Confusion' from which humanity will be able to emerge with the help of science and common sense.*

Then, I mean God help me. This is what comes into my head:

his sister, Minnie, sitting in the old armchair, glances up at him sitting on the arm of it next to her where he's poised waiting to be shown words. She shows him the spine of the book.

The Dream H G Wells.

She tells him it's a book about now, but that in it life right now is nothing but a dream.

Because the dream that the book is about, she says, is being dreamed inside the head of a person who's living two thousand years in the future from now!

Oh! he says.

She opens it at random. She points to a word far down on one of the open pages. The word is books. It's a word he knows.

Books, he says near her ear.
Good, she says.
She points to the same line further along.
Flow, he says.
Then he says
ers.
Yes, she says. But when you put those two together, it makes the word flowers. It's flow when you read it by itself, but with that ending it's more likely to be the word flowers than a word for things that are flowing like rivers.

Flowers, he says.
That's it, she says.
What's that word next to it? he says.
Try it, she says.
Flat. Ten. Ned.
The second e's a silent e, she says.
Flattened! he says.
Yes! Now. Try that whole sentence.
Books. Is. Flattened. Flowers. At. The. Best.
That's it! she says.
But why does it say *is* and not *are*? he says. Is that not wrong?

Yes. It's wrong. You're right. It should be *books are*. But the man who wrote this book thinks that if he uses *is* there, it'll look or sound more like certain people really speak. I think he believes that this is how common people speak. Or how he imagines people imagine they do.

Are we *not* common people then? he says.

We are, she says. We are uncommonly common, us.

But we don't speak like that. Or say is when it should be are, he says. Do we?

No. We do not, Min says. Do we?

No, he says. We don't do we? We is better than that.

His sister laughs.

We is, she says. Isn't we?

Well, I are, he says. You isn't.

I stop looking stuff up.

Not because I'm giving up looking but because the noise coming from the flat below mine right now is quite alarming. Tom downstairs, a man usually so quiet I sometimes wonder if I've even got a neighbour, has started making an almighty racket.

It's quite late. It's quite disturbing.

I'm beginning to wonder if everything's all right with him, the amount of noise he's making. It's like he's decided to shift the furniture from one room to another by throwing it. The last time we talked, about ten days ago, he seemed completely fine. He came to pick up a package left at mine for him when he was out, and standing at the door he told me he'd been to visit some caves in Italy.

You just can't believe your eyes, he said, I couldn't

believe it. It's very hard to take in, it's so enormous. Imagine a cave that's not just the size of a cathedral but is the size of St Paul's Cathedral twice over! Like if you were to stand one St Paul's Cathedral on top of another! Nobody knew it was there till some people were climbing some rocks one day and just stumbled on the place, they found a small hole in the rock surface, there was air coming out of it so they thought they'd found a cave. They dropped a rope down into it. But no rope they had was long enough. They had to get several more ropes and tie them all together. And Petra! It's so beautiful in there, beautifully lit. Everything looks like wax, like huge pipe organs in an amazing church, a church like the inside of a giant's body – like we were in the body of the whale like in the stories, like everything in there is candles, like rocks can melt. The stalactites! The stalagmites! The amazing size of them! I'm telling you, it puts time into perspective. I said to the guide, I pointed at a really small stalagmite, this size (he held up a finger and thumb about three inches apart) and I said, how long did that one take? and she said oh I'd say about a thousand. Days? Weeks? She meant years! Years! And the sizes of the others! Incalculable. Well, no, okay, easily calculable if you're a person who spends your time calculating the ages of stalactites and stalagmites in an expert way. But all the things that have happened on this planet since those great big stalactites and mites were once only this size. A mere thousand years old! Thousands and thousands and thousands of years. Telling you, Petra, what a lesson in the size of all of us.

And they say size doesn't matter, Tom, I said.

Ah, on that subject it's long been my opinion that us men just don't live long enough to mature, he said and winked at me.

Really, it sounds amazing, the place.

It was, he said. It is. What's more, it will be.

He waved the package in the air.

Thanks for this, he said. Sorry for the bother.

No bother at all, I said.

I like Tom. But I think I'm going to have to complain. I could be trying to sleep. There are other neighbours who will be trying to sleep.

There's also a strange smell like somebody burning peat, burning something natural anyway.

Maybe he's having a woodburner put in.

You can't carry out building work at this time of night. It's against the law.

My sister was saying something too muffled by the sound of the weather outside for me to catch.

Can't hear you, Patch, I said.

We were in our beds. It was dark. Rain was hitting the window hard.

She said it again.

Can't hear you. The rain, I said.

The next thing I knew she was across the room and climbing up on to my bed.

Couldn't hear what you said because of the rain, she said.

She started getting into my bed with me.

No way, I said. Get out.

Cold, she said.

She snugged herself down into it with her back pressed into my back.

Fuck off back to your own bed, I said.

I'll tell them you swore, she said.

I'll tell them you came over and attacked me for no reason in my bed and punched me in the head, I said.

They won't believe you, she said. You're in more trouble than me.

Not any more.

Hmph, she said because this was briefly true right then.

Pause.

Tell me more about when Glyph was a boy, she said.

No, I said. Go back to your bed.

Please, my sister said.

No, I said.

Just tell me something, one thing, she said. He wants you to. He wants me to tell you to tell me.

You're a deranged little weirdo, I said.

In what way am I the weirdo in this bed, a bed that does have a weirdo in it who isn't me? she said.

You're the weirdo, for doing things that a ghost who doesn't exist wants you to, I said.

She sat up. The covers came off me.

I know, she said. It's not like I don't know. I know it's just a story. I know we're just pretending. But I want to know what happens. And all he'll ever say to me in my version of him is that same word over and over and over, like his breath is getting squashed out of him and it's really sore that it is. It's quite upsetting. Actually I can feel myself getting quite upset by it right now. I think if you don't tell me something more about when he was my age that soon I will be really loudly upset.

You are unbelievably emotionally manipulative, I said.

I'm allowed to be, she said. I'm your younger sister. And you have to give in to me. It's written in the scars.

You mean stars, I said.

No I don't, she said.

No. You don't, I said.

We both laughed.

Shh, I said.

If you don't tell me I'll make a real noise so that they wake up and when he comes in I'll say you were frightening me by talking to dead people.

Is that a promise or a threat? I said.

Can it be both those things? she said.

You're a monster that's taken a human shape and is pretending to be my sister, I said.

You're a monster raving loony, she said. Everybody says so. Everybody at school. And when they do, what I do is I punch them in the mouth.

Is that why you punched that boy? I said.

Over the past couple of days my sister had been in big trouble at school and at home for hitting a boy from my class in the playground, two years older and much taller than her, hitting him in the face, giving him a black eye and refusing to say why.

Maybe, she said.

Did you hurt your fist when you hit him? I said.

I didn't use my fist. I used my schoolbag, she said. It had my lunchbox in it and in preparation for something like that happening, because people are always saying stuff about you now to me, I emptied what was in my lunchbox into my actual bag, it was all loose in the bottom of it, and filled the box with stones off the riverbank.

Patch, I said. That was stupid. You could've really hurt him.

I wanted to, she said.

You could've fractured his skull.

Nobody gets to say you're anything. Not to me. You'd do the same for me.

I wouldn't, I said.

Then I started laughing.

What? she said.

I've been wondering till now how you'd managed to reach up far enough to hit him in the eye, I said.

Easy. I just swung the bag hard in the air round my head and it hit him in the head, she said. Afterwards my sandwich had all pencil shavings stuck in it from the bottom of the bag.

Did you eat it? I said. Because lead is poisonous to humans.

No, she said.

Pause.
Well, I did, she said.
Pause.
Will I die? she said.
One day, I said.
Will I die of poisoning?
You'll go mad first, I said. And you'll froth at the mouth. You'll have to be injected in the stomach with huge needles.

Shut up, Petra, she said. I will not. Now you're actually seriously really frightening me.

What, more than ghosties?

Tell me. Please, she said. When I ask, it's just all glyph glyph glyph glyph glyph glyph glyph.

Maybe he's German and not English, I said. Maybe he's speaking in a language we don't know. Maybe he wasn't a man, he was a woman, or a little child who got really elongated.

No, she said. Look. I don't want any of those stories about those other people he might've been. Just do the story we were doing. With the sister who died, and the book and everything. That way he gets to be him, not someone else, or someone new.

Okay, I said. Let me think. Let me listen for a bit, see what he says.

I listened to the rain on the glass.

Then I said, do you know the story of the man at the cinema who taught him to draw birds?

No, she said. Tell me it.

Or do you want to know about the teacher who gave him a book when he left school when he was twelve?

Is leaving school at twelve even allowed? she said.

I don't know, I said. I know he had to leave because he had to earn money because his father died.

God. Everybody dies in this story, my sister said.

It's a ghost story, I said.

We both burst out laughing, then shushed ourselves. She put her head under the covers till she stopped laughing. The bed stopped shaking. She brought her head back out.

Where did Glyph go to work to earn money?

Uh. The ball bearing factory. Do you want to know about the ball bearing factory?

No, it sounds boring.

It's so not boring. It's like the most important industry of all the industries ever, and he worked there in it.

I don't care. Who was the teacher who gave him the book?

Okay, so she was a teacher who liked him and was sorry he was leaving and so she gave him one of her own books as a present. She'd taught his sister who died as well, and had made sure she'd got a scholarship to the grammar school because she was so clever. So she was sorry he was leaving, he was pretty sure she'd have tried to get him a scholarship too, because he was himself quite clever though not as clever as his sister.

Says who?

It's just a fact of life, Patch, that nobody is ever as clever as their sister.

If what you just said is true it also means *you're* not as clever as *your* sister.

Obviously the word sister here implies older sister. Older sisters are always cleverer. Anyway it turned out the book she gave him was a book that he couldn't read because it was in an English language from the past. But he managed to work out some of the story, about a green man on a green horse whose head gets chopped off but even so he doesn't die, he just picks his head up and tucks it under his arm, and it speaks from there under his arm to the king and queen and everybody.

I don't believe a word of it, my sister said. A chopped off head can't speak.

I think you'll find that in real history Mary Queen of Scots's head carried on speaking after they chopped it off, I said.

It did *not*!

It did. It's recorded.

There's a recording of it? Can I listen to it?

No, she died before that kind of recording existed. But it's written, in books about her. It says her mouth in her head kept moving and her lips kept speaking.

What did they say? Her lips I mean.

Nobody knows. I think that's because the axe will have gone right through her voice box so that would mean nobody would've been able to hear it anyway.

Do I have a voice box?

Yes. You're using it now.

Do we all have a voice box?

Yes, I said (though I'd no idea if we did or we didn't; for all I knew people might easily be born without a voice box). Except mute people, I added in case.

What's a mute person?

A person who can't speak.

Oh.

Pause.

What was the other story, about drawing, again? she said.

So, yeah, uh. The other story he told me is that there was a doorman at the cinema who taught him to draw birds.

What's a doorman?

I don't know. A man in a uniform. He also said this man only had one hand and one and a half arms, but that he was quite a good artist with the hand he still had. And that meant that your Glyph also got to be quite a good artist at drawing things. So much so that when he went off to war when he was a bit older, his mother gave him a letter to take with him that said don't let the gun mechanisms ruin your fingers for drawing.

And did they? she said.

Pause. Then she said,

oh yeah. Something did. Didn't it?

Flat hands, I said. Can't draw anything.

Yeah, but before that. Before it did. What did he draw? Do his drawings still exist? Are they somewhere where we can see one?

Uh . . .

I pretended I was listening for more information. I shook my head.

I'm not getting any answer, I said.

Imagine, my sister said. Imagine if we were just walking in a street one day and we saw a piece of paper in a gutter and we picked it up and uncrinkled it if it was screwed up and it had a picture on it and the picture was of a bird and it was a picture by him.

Imagine if we were in a museum or a gallery full of pictures, I said, and there was one by Anonymous and it was of a bird. And it was a really good picture, it was so like a bird that when we looked at it, it was like a real bird that could really fly was looking us right in the eye, in that way that the eyes of people and animals in some pictures can look the people looking at those pictures right in the eye and follow them round a room.

Yeah, my sister said. But not in a creepy way, right?

No, I said, more like it's saying the words hello! I'm not dead, I'm alive! How alive are you? And the card on the wall next to it telling people who come to the gallery about it says *nobody knows who this artist was but it is a really quite outstanding picture of a bird and though the artist who drew it is now lost to history this picture they drew is not lost to history*. And you and I looked at it, and we both knew.

We knew it was by Glyph, my sister said.

I nodded.

We did, I said.

Ted the doorman says it's pretty certain now that the Elite is shortly to be taken over by something called Associated British. Ted says he's shortly to be let go. Nobody wants a one handed man reminding people what people these days don't want to be reminded of.

I can still feel pain in it. It's there. Even though it's not, Ted says when he's had something to drink, which is the only time he ever talks about it.

It was Ted who caught him chalking the walls round the side of the Elite when he was a kid.

Don't just write your name on a wall like a mindless little reprobate staking your claim like a streak of dogpiss up a wall. What the bloody hell's that mean to anyone? Nothing. If you're going to leave a mark somewhere leave something a bit more imaginative than that, why don't you.

Tonight Ted glances out the nearest of the big doors after the queue's mostly gone, sees him there waiting and jerks his head, meaning come in too. He says something that makes the ticket sellers laugh as he goes past the booth. He opens the door behind the ticket office, switches the light on. It's warm in there. No window, no air. Ted takes off the peaked cap, shrugs off the greatcoat and hangs both on the back of the door, coat first, cap on top. He shakes his empty shirtsleeve at him to get him to sit down. He nods to him to sharpen the pencils; Ted likes there to be a row of ready pencils so he'll never have to be without a sharp one, and a one handed man can't sharpen pencils by himself.

He sharpens one then holds it up.

Sharp enough, Ted?

Mr Bartlett to you, Ted says.

The box office girls all call you Ted.

That's because they've licence to, Ted says.

How do I get one of those licences?

It helps if you're a girl working in the box office for a start, Ted says. Now. Concentrate. Remember. The line and the curve are like the bones of a drawing. Where two lines meet, or where a line crosses over itself, that's dimension, and dimension's what it's all about.

What's dimension, Mr Bartlett?

It's, it's.

Ted hits the table with his hand.

It's when something has solidity, he says.

Ted takes the pencil and checks the sharpness of its end with his thumb. He opens the notebook. It has printed lines on it for keeping your writing straight. But he acts like the lines aren't there. He draws an egg shaped circle. He draws another smaller circle resting on its top. He draws lines where a neck might be and triangles where legs might be and lines beneath it and running up one side of it for a tree branch.

He puts the pencil down, takes the rubber, holds the notebook down on the table with the elbow of his stump arm and rubs away the curves that cross over between the top circles. He opens up the top circle at one side with the rubber. Then he takes a different sharper pencil and draws three strong short lines like an arrowhead pointing away.

It's very nearly a beak on a bird, very nearly a bird on a twig.

Then very suddenly it couldn't be anything else.

You don't need much, Ted says, to show a life, or a world. Curve here, line there. Erase a little, add a little, there it is.

Ted finishes the bird, turns the page, pushes the notebook towards him instead and nods at the row of pencils.

He chooses one.

He does all the same things as Ted's done. Circle. Circle. Two lines, slight curve. Triangle. Slim triangle. Triangle. Rubber. Wipe shreds of rubber off the page.

Arrow for beak. Shade lines for feathers. Circle for eye. Circle inside it for light in eye.

Shade everything else in the eye circle dark.

Ted turns the page back towards himself.

Good. Good enough, he says. You're getting it. Now. You know the drill. Same drawing all over again. This time using your other hand.

Ghosts don't exist.
　They don't. End of.
　Story, however.
　It is haunting.
　Everything tells it.
　A single detail tells it endlessly, powerful how it does, how story moves through all the modernity in its ancient green clothes and shows up everything that thinks itself new as transparent, shambling, same old; story's as old as the hills itself and as brand new as everything that manages, against the odds, to grow fresh and new on those old hills.
　I am, I realize now, quite frightened at its wildness and its hugeness and its persuasiveness and pervasiveness.
　Perhaps my skin is thinner, after all, than everybody else decided it was.

Now I'm sitting on my couch in the almost dark. The only light in here, it'll dim in a minute or so, is off the laptop screen on which I've been trying to look up the real or not stuff.

Real or not's quite a good description of anything looked up online nowadays.

Maybe it's quite a good description of ever trying to look anything up full stop.

What's really real, though, is the smallness of a ball bearing and the massive pressure such a small thing has to be able to take.

I mean imagine a factory with its furnaces roaring, its steel coils chained and lifted and guided into the cutting machine, and that machine in turn spitting out roughly formed spherical chunks ready for the roar of the refining oven, and they get tipped into the grinder to smooth them down and that takes three days with the polishing barrels turning and turning them, and then, after the accuracy checkers have checked them to catch the wrong shape or size, because any single one of them that's out by the merest fraction means major disaster, the ones that pass the test are off to hydraulics to be tested for pressure. How high will they bounce?

That's the final check before they get passed down the lines to become tiny fundamental details in machine guns, small guns, big guns, gunships, tanks, submarines, planes, cars, all the engines ever, in fact any mechanical device, drones, phones, washing machines, toys, office stuff, home stuff, electronics of all kinds, missiles, bombs, always bombs – fundamental to all the wheels and all the cogs and all the machines and all the factories that make all these things, fundamental to everything of any real size that has moving parts, and not just fundamental to war, they're fundamental to all the industries. Not that there are many important industries left that aren't war industries – oh well, yes, fundamental too to oil and gas production at every level.

There he is, he's just turned thirteen. He starts as a coil guider helping chain up and hoist and swing the huge coils towards the cutters, but it becomes obvious pretty quick he's too small and thin for it so they shunt him into powdering where he tops up the containers with the unrefined spheres in them with ground charcoal, tamps them down, covers them, passes them on to Alfie the Heat whose job is to shove them with the shover into the mouth of the furnace and woe betide anyone who stands too near the flare.

Alfie the Heat.
Who the fuck's that?
Where did he come from?
Nowhere. But there he is, I can see him in my head. Handsome. Yorkshire-sharp. Bright as a cornfield. He looks like he'd be a good dancer. Foxtrot.

Also. How do I even know any of that ball bearing factory stuff?

Did I go away all the years ago and look it up somewhere, at a library, in an encyclopedia or some book I chose off a shelf, so I could provide some credible scenario for my little sister? This would explain why the factory in my head is quite old fashioned, less automated and has more actual people working in it hefting steel coils around than a fully automated one from now maybe would.

Could all be being done in a dark factory now I suppose.

Even the accuracy checking's probably done by machine.

I suppose I must've looked it up. How else?

Well. I meant well. It was nice of me, kind I suppose, at a troubled time, to do that.

I'll also for sure have been doing it out of self interest too, to smooth over difficult things for myself, get my own handle on them maybe.

I remember now that as soon as she died all the Glyph stuff just stopped.

It all disappeared.

We'd no further inclination or need for it.

More: it felt faintly obscene, now that we knew what death really was and loss really meant. For sure neither of us was ever tempted to go near some notion of our mother's afterlife or any faked contact with it, not even to go near the thought.

It was wrong. I assume Patch didn't go near the thought, or if she did I assume she knew how wrong it would sound out loud.

It would've been like charlatanning ourselves and our mother.

If charlatanning's a word.

So how come here's this story – including such a litany of ball bearing details as vivid as Alfie the Heat who features for a split second only in whatever this narrative is – opening in my head again so clearly?

And what's with the *woe betide*?

I mean I didn't even know I knew that expression.

Woe betide.

Who would ever use it?

Not me.

The last time we ever glyphed was probably the best time.

We were walking home from school.

We didn't usually walk home together from school. Usually we wanted nothing to do with each other round school.

It was sunny, warm, May, and we were walking home towards nightmare. Daytime was about to go dark and both daytime and dark were about to start to mean nothing. We didn't know it yet. We were together, at least, when we got home. But we weren't there yet.

Halfway there my sister started with the questioning.

Did he have a car? When he was old enough? Who?

You know. Did he?

I doubt it. They weren't well off after his dad died. Only well off people had cars then.

How do you know they weren't well off?

His mother and him lived in an old railway carriage on a piece of wasteland at the edge of the city.

They did *not*!

He says they did. He told me it was good, living there. Better than in a house. There were loads of doors and windows in the railway carriage, and several little rooms and a long corridor, so you could keep a small space quite warm, and there was privacy, and the seats still had cushions on them.

That's not anything like trains at all, she said.

It's like old trains were, before, I said. And it cost them nothing to live there, which was lucky because he wasn't making much at the factory. This was before he joined up.

Joined up what? All the little rooms in it?

No. Joining up meant be in the army or the navy etc. You got paid more than he did in the factory, and also, money got sent home to your mother if you joined up.

I don't care about that war stuff. I don't want to know about it. Did he have a girlfriend?

I don't know.

I bet he didn't. I mean, he lived in a disused railway carriage. Who'd ever go out with anyone who was living in a disused railway carriage?

Wait. I'll ask.

I stopped on the pavement, half-closed my eyes, started doing the pretend humming. A person coming towards us turned as she went past and stared at me. I ignored her. My sister tossed her a who do you think you're looking at look.

He did have a girlfriend, I said, and she liked the railway carriage. She said it was an ingenious way to live. She was a good sport.

What was she called?

Her name was Lena.

Lena.

Yes.

Was it Lena Gainst? Was it Lena Tower O'Pisa?

Lena Horn.

Lena Gainsta Horn! How did they meet?

She worked at the same factory as an accuracy checker. That was a really important job. She had some of the best eyesight in the country.

Only some of it? Who had the rest of it?

Ha ha!

What did Lena look like? she said.

I don't know. But.

But what? she said.

I have news.

What kind of news?

He also had a boyfriend.

No way!

Way, I said. And I found out that this was before

boys and men having boyfriends was legally allowed.

Why?

I don't know. But you could be put in jail for it or injected with stuff, like Alan Turing.

Who?

He was ultra clever, I said. He decoded things that won the war and he helped invent computers.

No wonder they put him in jail. So Glyph was a criminal too.

Yeah, but all in the cause of love.

My sister thought about it.

I'd be a criminal for love, she said.

Me too, I said.

What was his boyfriend's name?

Alec, I said. And he *was* quite well off. He was two years older and he got called up first.

On the phone? By Glyph?

No, stupid. Called up meant you had to go to war, you'd got sent your call up papers. You were enlisted. You got them when you were eighteen. I looked it up. You had to go, unless there was some health reason or you worked in a job that meant you were more necessary at home.

Yeah, but what did Alec look like? she said.

Ah. He says Alec was very handsome.

But which did he prefer? Lena or Alec?

I'll ask him, I said.

We stopped and sat on a low garden wall.

Ah. Okay. He says he loved them both equally but for different reasons.

Cop out, my sister said.

He just told me to tell you not to be rude.

Sorry, Glyph, she said to the thin air in front of us both.

Apology accepted. He says Alec went first.

What, died first?

He says he was on a ship and there was no news for weeks, just news of torpedoed ships going down. So he decided to try to find out by going to Alec's house to ask if his family had any news. But he'd never been to Alec's house, because he was a secret from everybody, and also because he wasn't the class of person who could go and just visit someone rich's house like an equal, you couldn't do that in those days, there were tradesman entrances you had to go to.

That is insane, she said. They are boyfriend and boyfriend. They love each other.

Apparently there'd have been big trouble if anyone'd found that out. For both of them.

My sister shrugged.

Lucky there's still Lena then, she said.

Anyway, there's this one evening, and it's the night before Glyph is off himself to the war, and he's meant to be going to the cinema with Lena. So he starts walking towards town. But.

But what? she said.

But he gets to a crossroads, I said, and instead of towards the cinema he finds himself going down a road in the opposite direction, towards where there are all these big houses where the rich people live.

He definitely prefers Alec, my sister said.

And he walks for ages, I said, and it's like the town, the city, is melting away behind him and everything is trees and clean air and neatness and you can see the sky for miles. He gets to a long and very tall stone wall, say about ten times the size of this one we're sitting on. He walks along the side of it for quite a long time. He can't see over it. It's way too tall to jump and catch the top with his hands and pull himself up to see over it. Then the wall gives way to an also really tall iron fence that's got big spikes at the top of it. So he knows these people must be really, really rich, because it says in the book I read about the war that people had to give up their metal fences to be melted down and made into weapons. But these people have somehow managed to keep their fence.

Is it Alec's house? she said. Is Alec there?

He gets to a gate in this fence. He holds two of the bars and he looks through them, like he's in jail and peering through. The front garden he's looking at is so wide you could fit the whole street he used to live on into it. One side is all dug up for growing vegetables. The other side is all lawn and the most amazing flowers all falling over themselves. The house ahead of him has a turret at one end.

Alec lives in a fucking castle, man, my sister said.

He just told me to tell you watch your language. He says the people in the house behind us will be offended if they hear you swear and will come out and ask us to get off their wall.

My sister rolled her eyes.

Go on, she said.

Then this happens. A huge white dog comes running at him as fast as out of a catapult barking like it'll kill him and he backs away from the gate just before it gets its nose through the bars and snaps its teeth really close to his stomach.

That's a pity, she said.

Why? I said.

If that dog had bitten his stomach he would have had to go to hospital and maybe he wouldn't have had to go to war in the first place and he would never have got flattened later.

And now a small girl about the same age as you, I said, is coming running down the garden. She's shouting a name at the dog.

Is the dog called Shandy?

No. Brandy. Its full pedigree name is Napoleon Brandy.

What's a pedigree name?

A posh name. Something to do with breeding.

And this girl, she drags it away from the gate by the collar and tells it to be quiet and to lie down. It does. It lies down at her feet. And she says – what does she say, Patch?

What d'you mean what does she say? my sister said.

You tell me, I said. What does she say?

Oh, okay. Uh, the girl says: it's okay. Napoleon Brandy is my mother's dog. She's not really frightening.

Right. And Glyph says through the gate bars: your mother's not really frightening?

And the girl says: I'm not talking about my mother. I'm talking about the dog.

That's good, I said. Go on.

And then, Patch said, she says: actually my mother can be really frightening too. Especially when she loses at golf.

What, your mother the archaeologist?

Oh no. My mother's not anything like whatever it is that you just said. She goes shopping. In London. She plays golf. She's very sporty. We have a small sports car and she drives it very fast. Is there something you want, Mr –

Glyph.

Should I call my mother or one of the servants? Are you sure you're even at the right house? You know, there are several other similarly large rich people's houses quite close to here. I fear you might be at the wrong house.

I'm here because I was under the impression that a friend of mine lives here.

Who?

Alexander.

Is that another name for Alec?

Yes.

Ah. Yes. Alec. He's my brother. He's not here. He's, you know. Away. At the war.

You look a little like him.

No I don't.

You do.

I really don't. He looks much more like my mother. I take after my father.

You know, I didn't know till now that Alec even had a sister.

You don't know much then.

I know some things.

Did you know he's away in a ship at sea?

Yes, I know that. I'm here because he is a dear friend and I wondered if you have any news of him at all.

(Do I?

No.

Okay.)

No, I'm sorry. We haven't heard from him.

Well. If you do hear from him, will you give him a message from me?

Yes, of course.

Right then. Tell him from me, uh, tell him.

Tell him what?

Tell him: Glyph you can keep your head when all about you are losing theirs and blaming it on you, you'll be a moon my sun.

(We heard someone behind us open a window and shout at us to move on.

We stood up off the wall, picked up our schoolbags and apologized in unison. We shouldered our bags and carried on along the pavement towards home.

Still be Glyph, she said as we went. And I'll still be the sister.

Okay, I said. So he's about to say goodbye to her at the gate with the spikes, okay?

Right, she said.

They used to say words like cheerio when they said goodbye. So that's what I'll say. Ready?

Ready.

Well, cheerio! Okay, so now I'm – I mean he's – walking away along the fence, going back the way he came.

Is he going to meet Lena at the cinema now?

Yes and he's quite late now and doesn't want her to be left standing by herself outside the cinema, and doesn't want her to have to miss the start of the film, so he's hurrying.

Okay, so now I'm running along the fence on the other side to keep up with him, yes?

Yes, and remember, the fence turns into a

stone wall quite soon, the really tall stone wall he can't see over. So you're on one side and he's on the other. Right. The fence has just turned into the wall. Shout something that'll catch his attention.)

Hey! Hey! Mr Glyph! I just thought of something!

What?

It's a poem! I made it up! About us!

What poem?

Here goes: are you ready?

I'm ready.

You're an enlister and I'm a sister!

Hey! Hey –

(uh, what's your character's name again?

I don't know.

Choose a high class name.

A pedigree name! What about – Celeste?

Yes. That's good.) Cheerio Celeste! All the best! Stay warm! Always wear your vest!

(Or no. I'm going to choose Cynthia. I'm choosing it on purpose because nothing rhymes with Cynthia.)

Cheerio Cynthia! See you when we win-thia!

(Ha ha ha!

Ah. Except he won't, though, will he?

No. He really won't.)

Hey! Mr Glyph!

What?

Take care of yourself! Look after your helf! Be unconventional! Stay three dimensional! Avoid combat! It'll leave you feeling flat!

Bye!

Bye!

(We were minutes from home and laughing so much now on the pavement that we fell against each other, had to hold each other up so that neither of us fell over.)

What to do about nightmare:
   can your sister hear? our mother said.
   No, I said.
   Are you sure? Is she asleep? Go and check. Go very quietly.
   I went to check. I came back.
   Yes, I said.
This happened years before all the Glyph etc stuff; I was still quite small, seven or eight, and I'd woken from a nightmare and found our mother sitting on my bed; she must have heard me wake up and shout something, make some kind of distressed noise, and she'd come through from her own room. I sat up straight into her warmth.
   What did you dream? she'd said. Tell me it very quietly so we don't wake your sister.
   I dreamed I was floating as loose as a loose

balloon in the air, I said, and there was nothing I was tied to, nothing at all. It was frightening. Then I dreamed that I myself turned into a balloon and that a child I don't know bought me at a fair and tied me to a railing that had sharp spikes on the top of it and left me behind and there was no way I could get free, and I had to try to keep myself up in the air above the spikes and not descend on to them so I wouldn't get pierced by them, and it was difficult because I wasn't helium, I was just ordinary air, I mean inside me.

That's quite a dream, she said.

She gathered me, arms and legs, up.

Come on. Come with me.

Where? I said.

To the stair on the landing, she said. It's nice there.

We sat together on the top step. The stairs continued down themselves below us. It was light outside through the landing window curtains though it was still the middle of the night, it must've been high summertime. She put her arm round me.

The floating was terrible. But the being tied was worse, I said.

Right, she said. If you ever dream that dream again where you're floating like that then tell yourself this: I am a free agent, and the great thing about floating this way and that, whatever way the wind is blowing me, means I can act like the weather and I am a part of the weather. And what's more I can now see and hear all sorts of things by chance that otherwise I wouldn't have seen or heard.

Oh, I said. But what about if I'm tied to a railing? And at any point might fall on a spike and it will go right through me and then I won't exist any more? I'll just be a shred of rubber on a string left hanging off a railing.

You're forgetting what's inside you, she said. All the air that makes you you, everything inside your skin, would be completely freed if that happened, so free it would simply join up with things so much bigger than it, you'd become a part of a huge communal mass of air unthinkable to a single balloon!

Oh, I said. That's brilliant. But can I ask a question about something else?

Always, she said.

Why don't Patch and I have grandparents? So many people at school have grandparents and we don't.

You do. It's just that they're dead now. But you still have them.

How?

In your DNA. In the cells of your body, the stuff that makes you who you are. My parents, your grandparents, died before you were born.

Like in a fairy story?

Well, yes, I suppose, quite like in a fairy story. There are photos somewhere. I'll look them out for you and show you. And there'll be photos of your father's parents, they're still alive. I only met them once. They didn't take to me.

Oh. Why not?

They thought your father was marrying down in the world. They thought I was the wrong class. They said my eyes were foreign looking. But they're your grandparents too. Maybe you'll get to meet them one day.

Will I?

Honestly? I hope not. I never want to see them again. But they're not my grandparents. They're your grandparents.

She laughed.

Listen, I'm the same as you, she said. My own grandfather and grandmother were gone by the time I was your age. But I do have this amazing true story to tell you, one from nearly a hundred years ago, it was passed down from one of them to my brother your uncle Ian, and then to me. It's a story your uncle Ian told me when I was your age, something our grandfather told him long before I was born, when Ian was the same age as you. Do you want to hear it?

Yes. But can I ask something else?

Always.

What is the difference between a fairy story and a true story?

Petra. What a question. Can I answer it after I tell you this true story?

Yes.

This is a story I can't tell your sister. It's a war story. She's too little for war yet. But you. You're different. You've a skin as thick as boot leather, haven't you.

Yes.

And the thing about any balloon with a skin as thick as leather. It'd bounce like a football unharmed off those fence spikes, so never worry. And it means I can tell you, because you know about difficult things like wars.

I only know about war from films.

Yes. Me too. So. Are you brave enough for a story you have to be a bit brave to hear?

I nodded.

She told me about a man her grandfather had said was the person of the highest and best qualities he ever knew in his life, a young man he fought alongside in the First World War who led a horse away from near a battlefield after he saw that the horse had gone blind because he didn't want anybody to shoot it now that it was blind.

Why were they going to shoot it? I said.

It was of no use to them now that it couldn't see.

Why did it go blind?

It was gas. Soldiers from different sides of the conflict were gassing each other and the horse got gassed too. The type of gas they used could make you go blind.

Why did they gas each other?

That's the kind of thing that people do in wars. But what I love about this story, Petra, is that the man knew that what was happening was wrong and that the horse had nothing to do with that wrong. So he took off all his soldierly kit and dumped it on the ground, and he took that horse by the forelock, you know what a forelock is?

Is it a kind of lock?

It's called a lock because it's a lock of hair, the long fringe of horse's hair that hangs down over its forehead between its eyes, and he took it in his hand and that's how he got the horse to go with him, and he went off with that horse into the woods and stopped being a soldier. So, you see, even when things are pretty dire, there's always something we can do, always a choice we can make, to make them a bit less dire.

Mum?

Yes?

Why does hair have locks?

I don't know. To keep people out of our hair? To stop people stealing it?

Does that mean bald people have been seriously burgled?

Shh, we have to laugh more quietly or it'll wake your sister and I don't want to have to deal with two of you at this time of night. One's more than enough. As I said to your father once. But did he listen? No. Thank goodness. Thank goodness he didn't. Now you and your sister'll always have each other.

Like you have a brother?

Well, yes. In the old days.

Don't you have him any more?

No, I still do. I always will. Family isn't always easy. But it's non-negotiable. As I suspect you'll discover, in time.

In time for what?

Just in time, passing.

And mum. If those were the old days. Are these the new days?

Come on. No more negotiating. Back to bed. I've to get up for work. You've to get up for school.

She stood up, picked me up, carried me round the stairturn towards my and my little sister's room.

We've had good talks. You'll sleep better now, she said.

Will I?

Course you will.

People were drinking in the front room with our father.

My sister was in the garden shed.

She'd gone out there the night our mother died and she'd refused since then to come back into the house for longer than it took to change clothes or get something to eat or go to the toilet. I'd been out once, to check she was okay. She was more okay than I was. She'd made a bed for herself by erecting a sun lounger down beneath the bike handlebars. This meant the door was blocked and that only she was now small enough to get easily into the shed.

I was sitting by myself in the kitchen on one of the hard chairs.

I was a felled and hollowed tree.

I was twelve years old.

The shy older man who'd brought the boxed up talking toys came into the kitchen.

Earlier, when we'd got home from the church, he'd got the boxes out of the boot of his car and he'd held them out, one to each of us. We'd each taken them, each said thank you and each put them straight down on the ground outside the house and left them there. Someone else had brought them in; they were there in the hall when everybody'd gone.

He poured himself a glass of water out of the tap and drank it over the sink. He turned round. He had the same eyes as our mother.

Are you our uncle Ian? I said.

I am, he said. You're Petra.

I am.

How are you doing? he said.

I'm okay. Can I ask you something? I said.

Always, he said.

He pulled out another of the chairs from the table and sat down. I asked him about the only thing I knew about him, the story he'd told our mother, our great grandfather's story.

Oh. The Sherwood Foresters, he said. The court-martialled boy. Yes.

He told me many things my mother hadn't told me in her version of the story.

Somebody shot him? I said. Dead? His own side?

Don't they teach you the First World War at school? A firing squad of British soldiers shot him at dawn.

For taking a horse away so *it* wouldn't be shot?

Well probably more for the desertion. For abandoning his kit, his duties and his battalion. The horse thing probably didn't bother them so much. But my grandfather, your great grandfather, believed he'd done the only right thing there was to do.

What happened to the horse? I said.

Our uncle did a double take, as if I was being stupid, smiled a sideways smile. Then he stood at the kitchen sink, washed the glass he'd used, then washed and dried what dishes were still in there from the past few days.

Right. I'm off now, he said. Your father has my address and my phone number. I wrote it in the address book by the phone in the hall too.

Under which letter? I said.

He looked surprised.

E.

What for?

For Eckman, he said. Don't you know? We're the Eckmans. Your mother was an Eckman. You're an Eckman too, as well as a Wild. Believe it or not, we're not just partly English, and somewhere back in time clearly also a little bit Indonesian, we're also part Scandinavian from back in the late 1800s.

That makes you, at least partly, a real northener. A viking. An explorer. A survivor.

I looked at the floor.

It didn't mean *she* survived, I said.

Yes she did, he said. She's here right now. In me, in you and in your sister.

He buttoned his coat.

You'll tell me if you ever need anything, he said.

He waited for me to nod. I nodded.

After he'd gone I studied the surface of the kitchen table. I wondered what happened to those people who didn't have children in whom they could be said to have survived when they died. Did that mean they died a double death, disappeared twice as hard, because there was nobody left to represent them physically in the world?

Meanwhile my sister caught sight of the talking toys in the hall next time she came in, got them out of their boxes and took them out into the back garden. She sat them on our father's compost heap, surreal little bright slabs of colour on top of all the thrown away flowers and food, where they fell over in the wind so that one lay face down, one lay with its legs and arms sticking up in the air, out in the rain for weeks.

Seeing them out there was the end of innocence. It meant that colour itself, along with the mass producedness of everything, became more disturbing, to me anyway, than honest rot.

    One day they weren't there any more.

    He threw them out, I guess. Someone must've. Maybe it was even me. If it was, I've blanked it.

I wake the laptop from its fairy tale sleep again.

I decide to try my luck at finding some reality in the other story, the one our great grandfather told, from the earlier war.

I type in *sherwood foresters first world war shot at dawn*.

The net comes up with lists and details, though it's not always clear whether these men are in the Sherwood Foresters or not.

Or maybe it's me who's not being clear and not looking at the information properly.

It's quite hard to concentrate with the noise Tom's making downstairs. It's like he's dismantling his own walls.

Anyway.

A lot of men, it's clear, were shot at dawn, hundreds of men.

I read what it says online about five of them.

One man kept going missing from wiring parties but turning up again for food. He was put in detention, which he escaped. They caught him six weeks later. They shot him. One man who was in trouble for drinking went missing and was found in a house in a nearby town still wearing his uniform but with all the military stuff stripped off it. They decided he was of sound enough mind to be shot. They shot him. One man told his soldier mates in 1914 that he'd hurt his leg and was going off to get it looked at by someone, after which he disappeared and wasn't found till two years later living in a house in a village with a French woman he was in love with. *No redeeming features were found to upset the sentence of death.* They shot him. One man failed to report back for fighting after a spell of leave in England, where he had a child with his girlfriend, infuriated his mother who didn't like her by marrying her, applied for more leave so he could *stand by the girl who was now my wife*, dealt with the dysentery he'd picked up in Gallipoli – several of the people executed seemed to have in common that they'd fought at Gallipoli, narrowly survived, then been shipped back to the Somme – and worked with his wife in Scotland on a farm until he got arrested by a local policeman, taken back to France for court martial, then shot.

Harry. Jimmy. Fred. Arthur.

A young man called William went looking for his younger brother after he heard that the battalion his brother was in was now fighting quite close to where his own battalion was. But when he came back from looking, his own battalion had moved on and the officers had registered him AWOL. He wandered around trying to find them till an officer spotted him, checked who he was and arrested him. He was put in detention for three months, then a Brigadier General called G F Trotter declared *an example should be made* of him and *the extreme penalty should be carried out.*

He was the eldest of five children. The youngest brother of the five of them had died in 1901 barely a year old when William was seven. He'd been twenty or twenty one and working in the mines when war broke out. He enlisted at the very beginning and was sent to Gallipoli where *one of his first tasks was to bury mounds of British corpses 'rotting under the Turkish sun'*. He was wounded at Suvla Bay in August 1915, they shipped him home to England to recover, and he did, so much so that he was back in France on the battlefield on the first day of the Somme. A month later, having so far come through the Somme alive, one day he went looking for his brother.

His service number was 13167. *Commonwealth War Graves grave number: 587627. Tenth Battalion*

Sherwood Foresters. Born in Nottinghamshire. Date of death 25 Nov 1916. Age: 23.

Employment, education or hobbies: In 1911 he was a pit pony driver.

Down the mines from thirteen years old.

Why did they blindfold the people they shot at dawn? Was it for the benefit of the people being shot or the benefit of the people who were shooting them? Was it so that nobody in the firing squad would be faced with seeing someone they were shooting looking them in the eye? Was it to alleviate the guilt or shame that might be felt by the people doing the shooting? Did mandatory blindfolding mean that people could more easily, less disturbingly, be shot?

Were the people who were being shot given a choice: blindfold or no blindfold?

If not, did the fact they'd been disallowed sight make them symbolically not really there, already a kind of removed, already in darkness, already ceremoniously marked as a kind of dead?

Was it to signify the end of any day ever dawning

on them again? As well as quite practically to disempower them further, because hands tied behind their backs round a post wasn't disempowering enough? A safeguard so they couldn't or wouldn't struggle or turn their heads accusingly away from or towards anyone at seeing rifles being raised?

They'll have heard the commands.

Even such a short time of being blindfolded would've enhanced their hearing.

They'll have heard the slight shifts in the clothes and the stances of the people about to shoot them.

My doorbell goes.

Who's that at 11.45pm? Nobody comes to the door at this time of night.

I go into the hall and check through the little glass spyhole.

It's my downstairs neighbour.

I open it smiling, expecting he's come to apologize profusely for the noise.

Instead he looks angry. He says,

Petra.

Tom, I say.

Do you think, he says, can you maybe just stop making all the noise? It's nearly midnight now.

Me? I say.

It's like you've got a bloody elephant in there stamping on my ceiling, he says. We're sitting watching the lampshade tassels on the big light in my back room literally shaking.

It's not me making a noise, I say. It's you that's making the noise. I was literally about to come down myself and knock on your door about it.

Don't play silly buggers with me, he says. Really. I've got my daughter and one of the grandkids staying tonight. That's complicated enough without the bloody timpani. Just, whoever you've got in there, or whatever you're doing. Knock it off for the night now. Yes?

He turns and shambles down the stairs in his pyjamas.

What the fuck, Tom? I say.

Tone it down, okay? he shouts without turning round.

Gosh.

Tom must be losing his mind.

I shut my door and stand in the hall for a bit like I don't know what to do with my own arms.

The banging noise continues, random sounding thumps. The smell in my hall is even stronger, rotting flowers, rotten flower water.

I go back through. I switch the light on and stand in the living room.

I wonder if maybe the noise is coming from people doing something at the back of the building.

I decide I'll try and have a look out of the bedroom window, see if I can see anything down in the back gardens.

It's quite hard to open the door of the bedroom. I'm having to push against something. Even when it's open just a crack the stench comes at me really grassy and strong.

I put my whole weight against the door. I reach in and switch the bedroom light on.

There's a horse.

It's in my bedroom.

It has wrecked my room.

One bedside table is on its side. The other, fallen forward, is what I've been pushing the door against. The lamps are toppled on the floor. One cupboard has fallen open and everything that was in it is all over the place; there's spilt moisturizer from a split plastic container spreading all over the rug next to the bed, what looks like broken glass at the skirting board from the fall of a picture. Everything that was on the desk is also now on the floor and the desk is askew, and that desk is pretty heavy to have been knocked that much askew. The chair is flat underneath. The big bookcase has fallen forward against the desk and all the books have fallen out of it and are scattered across the floor.

The horse is grey and either has a lot of black markings or is pretty filthy. It raises its head like it scents me. It lurches in my direction.

But it crashes right into the side of the bed, bumps its forelegs, scares itself, stumbles back away and thumps its hind quarters on the wall behind it. This knocks another of the pictures off the wall; it falls and hits the horse on its flank and gives it another fright. The horse stumbles forward shaking its head from side to side and bashes its muzzle off the wardrobe door. One hoof slips on a paperback book under it. This startles it even more and it thuds itself backwards again and ends up funnelled in a space between the wardrobe and the bed.

Its ears are flat back, flat to its skull. It raises its nose, nods and nods its head in the air as if to shake itself loose from something.

Then very suddenly it calms down. It drops its head low. It stands still. It wheezes.

It brings its ears forward, towards me.

It's quite a small horse. Or quite a large pony.

Its flat bone forehead under its forelock makes its whole head appear like a ceremonial bone mask of a horse.

Its eye isn't like an eye should be. It's pale yellow, filmy, gelatinous.

Though it can't see me it's looking right at me.

What to do now?

Look up on the internet *what to do if you inadvertently raise a ghost*.

Really, Petra? That's your only option?

It's my most immediate option.

I close the bedroom door. I retreat to the front room. I find my phone. I try typing words in. I have to keep correcting them because my hands are shaking.

I correct advertly to inadvertently.

A lot of things come up about Airbnb hosts.

I add a g to the word host in the search bar and search again.

TikTok has many people's faces very close up offering tips and rituals. One involves asking God to forgive you because the ghost is a form of sin.

Under **People also ask,** Google says *Confront the ghost: Ghosts lose their potency when confronted head on. Similarly, facing your resentments is crucial for letting go. If possible communicate your feelings with the person involved or seek closure within yourself.*

I amend my original request:
what to do if you inadvertently raise the ghost of a horse.

Some games come up in which people have to solve something and if they can they get to ride the ghost horse. A site called Human Amplified offers to teach me the difference between spirits and ghosts. It tells me a lot about humans, Christianity and fictional characters. Nothing about a ghost horse that wrecks a bedroom.

I click on a site called Ghost Horses but it's about something to do with breeding practices so that your foals will have certain markings rather than about horses that are ghosts.

Meanwhile I can hear the horse is starting to shift round the room again.

Maybe if I open the door I can persuade it to be calm rather than to wreck anything else.

I do it. I go back across the room and the hall and I push the door open again.

There's still a horse.

Now it has its back to me. It seems to be chewing one of my jumpers. It hears me. It stops shifting around, turns towards me with the jumper hanging out of its mouth.

I say to it, because it can't see,

hello. I'm Petra. I don't mean you any harm. I'm going to come towards you now and take that jumper out of your mouth because I don't think you should be eating wool.

It doesn't flinch when I approach it.

You hungry? I say.

I put a hand towards its muzzle, to next to its nostrils; I've read something somewhere recently that told me that this is how you say hello to a horse.

Then I put my hand to its neck so it knows where I am. I take and hold the jumper. It lets the jumper go.

The jumper's covered in horse saliva.

I leave my hand flat on its neck, warm under my hand. It lets me.

Both its eyes are whitened, like they're sealed inside wax.

The hair on its long nose is patchy. It stoops its head to the carpet and runs it across the spilt books from the bookcase as if perusing for grass.

Okay.

I sit on the end of my bed and listen to the horse next to me blowing air out through its wet nostrils.

I phone my sister's number.

It's late. The answerphone kicks in.

Hi again, I say. It's me. Yeah, I know. Wait eight years for a phonecall then two come at once. I uh seem to have just really smashed up everything in one of the rooms in my flat.

Can you maybe call me back? As soon as you get this message?

wink

Here's the story of the day Patricia goes to the police station to pick up Bill.

What exactly has she done? Patricia says.

She was apprehended for waving a scarf in a markedly aggressive manner, Mrs, uh, Ms Wild.

You can't bring in and detain someone for waving a scarf, Patricia says. It's not against the law to wave a scarf.

Scarf waving is not in itself a specific criminal offence unless the waving of a particular scarf relates to a proscribed organization, Ms Wild. It was thought that the scarf waved like a flag by your daughter could have been said to be in tacit support of a newly proscribed organization and officers at the scene must now consider any individual or organizational gesture towards this new proscription in that light. In this instance as it happens the scarf your daughter was waving has been judged not to have been being directly used in support of the said proscribed organization. But it also says here that the officers present judged that your daughter's intent could be said to have been hostile.

Could be said to have been. Isn't that a bit subjective to result in the detaining of a sixteen year old girl? Patricia says.

It's her very good fortune that taking into account her clean record and her status as a minor the WPC towards whom she used verbal abuse and the threat of assault with the scarf has chosen not to press charges.

Right, Patricia says. Well. Thanks, thanks very much. Where's she now?

If you take a seat, Ms Wild. Someone will show you through in a moment.

The reception officer hands Patricia a ticket with a number on it.

Police property store, he says.

Thanks, she says.

(Did that reception officer just wink at her? Surely not.)

What exactly did you do? Patricia says.

I did nothing, Bill says. I did pure zilchio.

Patricia is driving them both home. Bill shakes her head and looks away out the side window.

I just stood there, she says. I was just, you know.

She turns her head back towards Patricia.

Present.

Present. That's a bloody irony, Bill. That you bunked off school is bad enough, Patricia says. I spent half an hour on the phone getting lectured about and covering for your chronic absenteeism today.

It was only PE, Bill says. I missed fuck all. And if they hadn't picked me up I'd have got back easily in time for Britain's Place in the World since 1945.

Is that History?

Oh yeah. It so bloody is, ha ha, Bill says.

I'm serious. You can't keep on being absent from school.

I only don't go to things I'm certain I don't need to learn, Bill says.

There's no such thing as something you don't need to learn, Patricia says.

Oh yes there is.

No, there isn't. Where did you go today instead of the school you were meant to be in?

I told you. I just went and stood outside the supermarket on Broad Street. I thought it would be good to be somewhere people were going in and out through doors that mechanically open and close by themselves, Bill says.

And all you did was wave a scarf?

I didn't wave anything. I just stood. I was just holding it, I didn't even hold it up, I'd taken it out of my pocket thinking I'd put it on and I was holding it like this because I was changing my mind, because the weather was too warm for me to wear it. I didn't even say anything out loud. And some people, quite old people, came out of the supermarket, nodded to me and stood with me. So we literally just stood there. Then the policewoman and the policeman crossed the road, asked us if we had a permit and said we were in breach of the peace because more people than were allowed to gather if we hadn't applied for a permit had gathered. They said we were interfering with infrastructure. But we were just literally standing there.

How many people?

Four. Five including me.

Did they arrest the other people?

I don't know. The woman standing next to me told them it was a public highway and we had a right to be there.

Where did you get the scarf from?

The protest I went on.

When was that?

Two Saturdays ago.

You went on a protest? To London? Without telling me? Patricia says.

Damn. They kept my scarf. Well. I'll get another one.

Patricia puts her hand in her coat pocket and takes out a plastic bag. It's sealed. Inside it there's a folded swathe of material.

Oh. Great. Thanks, Patricia, Bill says.

Not that I approve, Patricia says. I don't. Flag waving of any kind is a mug's game.

It's not a flag, Bill says.

Don't do it again. Not that I'm telling you you're not free to make your own choices about your own actions.

Yes you are, Bill says. You literally just told me not to do something.

And don't thank me, thank the British Constabulary for letting you off with a warning.

   Letting me off! I didn't do anything wrong! Bill says.

   No, you've definitely got off lightly. From what they told me it sounds like there could've been a verbal assault charge against you. And apparently you also assaulted one of them with that scarf.

   I did not! Bill says. I just wouldn't let go of it when she tried to take it. And my God! Verbal assault! I just asked her what did she think about people when they were queueing for food being shot in their hands, thighs, eyes or buttocks. I mean I said the word buttocks and she and the male officer exchanged glances and then she actually started laughing, they had to sort of hide their laughing.

   Patricia slams the brakes on so suddenly that the car stalls and the car behind has to brake. Its driver leans on his horn. She waves out of her window to the driver in it to pull past them. She apologizes to him through the window. Then she restarts the car, pulls in and parks it where they are, half up on the pavement and half off.

   She cuts the engine.

   She turns to Bill next to her.

   They laughed?

   At the word, Bill says. They had to stop themselves, straighten their faces, and then I saw it dawn on her, she had this look like she'd got something she could finally charge me with, like *okay good, this kid's said something that I can report as obscene.* You know by the way, Patricia, that you're committing an illegal act yourself, by parking this badly?

Patricia shakes her head.

Sweet heart, she says. Awful stuff happens to people all the time. You can't take it on board for them. Nobody can. You'd go mad.

We have to, Bill says. Otherwise we're, like, I don't know.

What? Patricia says.

Dead? Bill says.

Tell me everything that happened when they took you to the station, Patricia says.

Nothing to tell, Bill says. They put me in the back of their car. The doors in it had no handles on the insides. They filled out a form and put me in a room with no windows. A woman came and sat with me while I was in there. Then they came and told me they weren't pressing charges and I was getting off with a warning and that you were here to collect me.

And that's it?

That's it.

Bill shrugs.

Here's a transcript of some of what did happen when they took Bill to the station:

Appropriate Adult: [saying nothing, keying something in on iPad. On her lanyard it says the name Samantha]
Bill: Can I ask you something?
AA: Go ahead, uh – [looks at iPad, scrolls it] – Billie.
Bill: Do you ever wonder whether because of the covid time and the numbers of people reported dead every day then a lot of people now maybe don't care in the same way they would've done before it about how many other people die or are dying wherever, whyever or whenever?
AA: [blinks. Looks down at iPad. Scrolls] Uh . . .
Bill: So this morning. Did you hear on the radio about the people queueing for food and the snipers shooting at them and how the snipers doing this aren't only

shooting at people randomly, they're also playing a kind of shooting game? So some days they shoot the people in the hands, some days the chests, some days the heads? Some days they shoot people in the thighs, some days they aim for people's eyes, some days for people's buttocks?

AA: [suddenly flusters, taps things into iPad]

Bill: *Leaking faecal matter.* That's the term the journalist used. So. I looked up the word faecal. I didn't know what it meant. Then there were the people on the radio saying the journalist was lying and that it was fake information and wasn't happening. It's not like I'm a normal thrower-upper or anything, I mean there are a few of them at school, there are thousands of people telling people how to do it on the net, but I don't do it, it's not something I do. Anyway this morning I did – I threw up. I went to the bathroom and it just came up out of me.

AA: [taps iPad] Is it possible that you're pregnant, Billie?

Bill: Wow. Is that what you just wrote on there, the word pregnant? Aw. Man. No. I can't be. I haven't had sex with anyone male. Do you not get it? It was the word faecal. It was finding out what it means. And because the journalist said that you wouldn't die immediately, you'd die some days later of infection from leaking faecal matter. That's why. How them doing that thing connects the word human to the word shit. But I think partly I was also sick because of the pile on, the people saying it wasn't true, because

I also saw how, like, there's this huge mechanism and it's acting on everybody. It is such a simple mechanism it is actually stealthy brilliance. You just say something that's the truth is a lie. Or that something that's a lie is the truth. Then the matter of something being true or not stops being about truth or lies and becomes about choosing a side and it drops itself like a blanket over everything, a blanket the size of the sky – no, maybe more like a net, like a gigantic fishing net, or the kind they use to drop over people on game shows on TV, something quite difficult to get untangled from so you have to struggle against it just to get yourself to the place where truth is.

AA: Are you sure you're telling me the truth about not being pregnant, Billie?

Bill: See what I mean? It is like it is purpose-designed to be a truth killer.

AA: [keys things into iPad]

Bill: Did you just write something about me on there again because I used the word killer?

AA: No, no, Billie. Not at all. I was just making sure this machine's actually working.

Bill: And since we're talking machines here.

AA: Are you suggesting I am a machine that can talk, Billie?

Bill: No, no, not at all, I mean both of us. Well, me. Since I'm talking about machines. Do you ever wonder why we're always giving human names to machines, I mean like the machines that we ask questions to and that talk back to us? And to things like vacuum cleaners? And do you think it could be in any way related to how actual real people can be treated like they're *not* humans?

[Pause]

AA: Your theories are very lively for someone so young, Billie.

Bill: I'm sixteen.

AA: But just to reiterate. This isn't an interview, Billie. I'm not here to interview you about any whys or wherefores or anything. And Billie, you know you don't have to speak or explain or say anything to me. I'm just here to wait with you in this room until your parent or guardian arrives and then to assist you throughout the procedure, should there result in a procedure, in your communications with the police, whilst respecting your right to say nothing unless you want to.

Bill: No. I want to. The thing is, I am actually finding I have loads to say right now.

AA: That's fine, Billie. And I'm here to safeguard your interests, Billie, and to help you understand your rights and ensure those rights are protected and respected.

Bill: Samantha, I appreciate that, Samantha.

AA: Is that you pointing out that I say your name when I'm speaking to you, Billie?

Bill: Maybe, Samantha.

AA: I'll explain about why I keep saying your name. It's part of my training, the training they give us when we go through the process of qualification to become appropriate adults, often to use the name of the person we're assigned to accompany as their assigned assigned appropriate adult.

Bill: That's okay. It's a nice thing, to. I'm sorry if you thought I was being sarky. I am actually just a person super interested in the way we all use language.

AA: You're very earnest, Billie.

Bill: Thank you, Samantha. I'll take it as a compliment.

AA: What I mean is. You're very uh politicized for someone so young, Billie.

Bill: You're very politicized too, Samantha. We all are.

AA: I wonder what you mean by that, Billie.

Bill: To mean or not to mean. I mean, that's the question.

AA: Oh, very clever, Billie. I see what you did there.

Bill: What I mean is, I think you thinking and saying that I'm politicized is actually quite a politicized thing to do too.

AA: [face completely blank] As I already made clear to you, I'm not here to ask questions or answer questions about what you may or may not have done, Billie. I'm just here right now simply to accompany you in this room and make sure you're all right whilst we wait for your parent or guardian, who is, it says on here, apparently on the way.

Bill: Thank you, Samantha. Can I ask you something else?

AA: [looks uneasy, glances at clock on wall] Go ahead, Billie.

Bill: You know how we've been talking about machines? Can I ask you person to person what you think about how a lot of inhumanizing stuff is now happening everywhere now all the time? Including, in quite a stealthy way, in countries where people still believe they can be totally unaffected by any of the wars that are currently happening?

AA: I wonder what you mean by stealthy, Billie.

Bill: Okay. So. There's this girl called Olivia in our friendship group at school and her father died in January, and her mother got all these condolence messages on Farcebook from all her friends on there.

AA: Farcebook. You mean Facebook?

Bill: Yeah. We all call it that now in our friendship group. Because, listen to this. Later, when her mother met one of the people in the street, someone who'd sent her a condolence message, a really lovely one saying how much they sympathized, the person who'd sent it had completely forgotten or maybe hadn't even really realized that her husband, Olivia's dad, had died, and they asked after him and were really shocked to hear he'd died. That's sort of what I mean. I've also had it, I don't know about you, Samantha, with the gang of dictatorial old men running – by which I mean ruining – the planet. Like they're CGI dinosaurs, shaking it in their paws every day like it's their personal post-history snowglobe.

AA: [taps something else into iPad. Glances surreptitiously at clock on wall]

Bill: Can I ask, am I allowed to ask, about how you yourself are feeling about how the world's going right now? Or aren't appropriate adults allowed to comment? Can we maybe have a proper conversation? A really appropriate one? Because I'm beginning to think that dialogue might matter more than anything else in the world right now, and above all I don't want to be inappropriate. I want always to be, I'm very keen to be, someone who's responding appropriately to things myself. That's why I was so alarmed at finding myself throwing up this morning. Was that appropriate? It felt appropriate. It felt like it was the most appropriate thing I've done for, well, I think ages.

AA: [closes eyes as if sore, opens them wide, looks at ceiling. Blinks. Settles herself in seat. Settles cardigan. Glances at clock one more time]

I'll drop you off here, Patricia says when they pull up outside the house. I've asked Irina across the road to do you a baked potato if you need anything for supper, okay?

Bill unclicks her safety belt and opens the car door.

Thanks. Where are you going? she says.

My sister phoned me last night late. I'm going to drive over to see her.

What sister? You don't have a sister, Bill says.

Oh yes I do.

That's impossible. How can I have lived this long with you and not known about a possible aunt?

Maybe because in real terms you haven't lived that long after all, Patricia says. And I may be your parent-or-guardian at the police station but it doesn't mean you know everything about me.

Or anything at all apparently. Where does the brand new sister live?

London.

What! Bill says. An hour away and I've never met her! Wait. Is this sister an invention? Are you making up a pretend family because you're having an affair with someone you don't want to tell me about?

I wish. And you *have* met her, Patricia says. You were seven or eight. You met her after my father died and we went to clear his house before we sold it, you came with me on the days that weren't school days. You met her a few times before that, too, at various things. You were much smaller then, though.

I remember there was a garden and you showing me the shed and telling me you slept out there when you were my age, Bill says.

I was a little bit older than you were then, Patricia says. I was ten when my mother died.

I remember there was a loft and a ladder that went up into it through a hatch, and you had to pull the ladder down with a stick, I remember that.

Oh yes. The loft, Patricia says.

I don't remember anyone else being there when we were there, Bill says.

No, she *was* there, Patricia says. But we weren't exactly speaking at that point. We spent most of the time in different parts of the house from each other. Except when we went up to the loft. Up in the loft we had the most almighty falling out.

Why?

She was succinctly horrible. Not just her. I was too. So we went our different ways. It was better to. It happens.

But what if she's really horrible again today when you get there? Bill says. Or difficult? Or demanding? Or troublemaking?

She may well be all those things, Patricia says. Anything's possible with Petra.

Weird name.

I'll tell her you think so, shall I? Patricia says.

Is she older or younger? Is there a big age gap between you and her?

She's two years older. We were very close when we were small.

Has she got kids? Bill says. What does she do now?

She doesn't have kids, not that I know of anyway.

How can you not know whether your sister has kids or not? What kind of a family *are* you?

We seriously lost touch, Patricia says. It just happens that way sometimes. She told me last night she broke up with her partner after covid, a lovely person, I met her a couple of times, they were together for decades, met at university. She did a degree in archaeology and anthropology and got a high up job in management in a clothing company.

The partner? Bill says.

No, my sister Petra. But the clothes company went bust in covid and all its shops shut.

That'll be why they broke up, Bill says.

I don't know why they did, Mrs Novelist Detective. I don't know much about her life right now. Except that she's doing something to do with ENT.

What's ENT?

Health. Ear, nose and throat, Patricia says.

Patricia?

Uh huh.

What did you do at university again?

Literature. Language. Stop asking questions. I have to go.

Why are you going to see her now when you haven't for so long?

Yeah, well. She sounded like she really needed some help, Patricia says. Bill. Out. Come on. I've got to get on the road before the traffic.

What kind of help? I can help, Bill says.

It sounded psychological, Patricia says. If you know what I mean.

Is she the reason you went out and slept in that shed for all those months when you were a kid? Bill says.

Oh no. Not at all. We were best of friends then, Patricia says. But funnily enough, me sleeping in the shed features in one of the many stories going round in my head right now centrally featuring your possible aunt Petra.

What stories? Bill says. Tell me one.

Ha. Well. One day.

No, *now*.

No. I'm off. If I'm not back tonight, go across and sleep at Irina's.

No.

Well, that's up to you, Patricia says. And go to school tomorrow. Or it's not just you who'll be in trouble. I'm already in trouble, number of times I've had to bail you out. If you need anything ask Irina. If you need me voicenote or text me.

Can't I come with? Bill says.

No. You've school, Patricia says. And honestly, Bill, it sounds like she's been having a very rough time. I don't know what she'll be like with a stranger. It might just be easier if it's just me.

Bill shuts the car door with herself still in it and belts back in.

I'm not a stranger, she says. I'm her possible niece.

No, Patricia says. Out.

Tell me one of those stories about this mystery sister first, Bill says. Tell me about the last time you saw each other. Then I'll go.

Well, Patricia says. The last time I saw her I thought I was dreaming. But I wasn't. It was when she broke into our house.

She what? Bill says.

We hadn't spoken to each other for about a year,

Patricia says. Then one night when I was sleeping, you were sleeping too, you were still small, she got into the house and she stole something from me. Something that had belonged to my mother.

What?

A sewing case. I more or less saw her do it. I was like, oh my God, is that my sister? Crossing my room like a ghost?

I'm sorry, she stole a *what* case? Bill says.

Patricia laughs.

A stupid plasticized sewing case, she says.

Here's what Patricia isn't saying out loud here:
   I see her – or I dream that I see her – bend down at the side of my bed like she's kneeling to say a childhood prayer kind of thing.
   She's come for the case, I think in my dream.
   But in the morning when I wake up and remember and check to see, the sewing case is still there under my bed.
   So it *was* a dream then.
   I get up. I get Billie up for school. I do all the things mornings demand. I go to work.
   That afternoon when I get home I feel uneasy and I can't think why.
   I come back upstairs and unzip the case and peel its lid back just to take a look at what's in it again. Not that I've opened it once, not since I took it home and put it under the bed.

This is what I find in there.

All the cotton reels have been sliced down their middles.

The pairs of scissors each now only have one arm.

A tape measure is as long as it always was but only half as wide. A clean long cut all the way through it lengthwise has been done with real care.

The white chalky stuff for marking up material has been chopped down its middle.

The sheaf of paper patterns, guillotined.

There's is only one of each size of knitting needle.

Two wool balls sit like halved fruits on the floor of the case as if their other halves are in the process of passing right through it.

I realize I am holding up exactly half of a little packet of needles and turning it in the light at the window in my bedroom like it's an artefact, an artwork.

It will have taken a lot of strength or an exceptionally sharp blade to cut through the thimble.

It will have taken some ingenuity to part the scissors' arms so cleanly from each other without warping the arm left behind.

She will have come into my room twice at least without me knowing, then. Once to take it. Once to put it back.

Oh my God. The person who did this to these things is my sister.

That sewing case: it was just a plasticized case, two feet long, a foot wide, half a foot deep. It isn't even something I ever saw my mother using; she wasn't a person who ever sewed things, at least not in any of my memories of her.

We're in my father's house after his funeral throwing everything out so we can put it on the market, and I suddenly remember the hatch in the ceiling above the landing and wonder if there'll be anything in the loft to throw out too.

I go out to the shed and fetch the long stick with the hook on its end that they always used to unlatch the hatch. It's still there where it's always been, hanging on the nail to the side of the door. I wipe off the cobweb and the grime. I come back in with it and up the stairs and I undo the catch. The hatch falls open. I use the hook to pull down the ladder.

My sister is downstairs emptying things from the kitchen cupboards into black plastic bags. She will have heard the ladder thunk down. We are already on no-speaking terms. But from nowhere she appears at the foot of the ladder to hold it steady as I go up.

When I get to the top I swing myself on to one of the boards over the rafters and hang my legs out of the hatch. I feel in the air for a cord I seem to know will be there, not that I remember going up into the loft ever before.

I pull it. Light.

Oh. What on earth? I say.

My sister comes halfway up the ladder.

Everything that belonged to my mother is up there mixed and muddled, all just lying around. Spilt clothes. Blouses and dresses and coats, and her shoes all over the place. Scarves, winter hats. A glove. Her underwear, her bathrobe, her books and magazines. Her make up, lipsticks loose like they just rolled across the floorboarding a minute ago, a petrified bottle of moisturizer. A splayed pile of the LPs she particularly liked; he'd removed them from the shelf and left only the ones that were originally his. Stacks of old videos. A mess of personal papers. Pictures she'd liked. Her gardening books and secateurs and twine and gloves. A mug.

One day a few weeks after she died Petra and I had come home from school and everything still belonging to her, anything to do with her in the house, had vanished. The living room windowsill was bare. The fiddler figurine with the line of a poem written on the pretend rock he stood on, *folk dance like a wave of the sea.* The glass duck with the grainy stuff painted on it that turned blue if the weather was going to be good and pink if bad weather was coming. Gone.

We'd got used to it not being there. It didn't take

long for me to, there wasn't much out in the shed to make me think of my mother. There was the smell of damp wood. There was the comfort of no comfort.

But all those things we'd thought gone. They aren't gone at all. They're all here, been here all the years without us knowing, just above our heads.

It is all just so much sad junk.

My sister comes up a couple of steps, stands between my hanging legs and sticks her head through the hatch to have a look. We've been being stony with each other. This is physically the closest we've been for a long time and I can feel we're both feeling the strangeness in it.

She scans the loft from side to side and nods airily like some kind of expert.

No wonder, she says.

No wonder what? I say.

The house never stopped having the scent of her, she says. All these years.

I have no idea what she means.

I sniff the air.

I can't smell anything.

Right then my hand is resting behind me on something, anything, in among some of the things closest to the hatch.

It's a brown soft plastic case of some kind. I close my hand round its handle.

I'm having this, I say. This is mine.

Plasticized. Sewing. Case.

Bill is sitting next to her in the car saying the words like they're the unlikeliest words for anyone ever to want to put together.

Why would you even want it? Bill says. You never sew. You hate sewing.

Patricia shrugs.

It belonged to my mother, she says.

Your mother who died that way you told me about.

By mistake. Too many sleeping pills. No one could wake her up, Patricia says as if reciting.

Like a terrible fairy tale you're trapped in and you can never get to the end of, Bill says.

They exchange a look. Patricia widens her eyes at Bill, says nothing. Bill nods, says nothing. They both look straight out through the windscreen at nothing.

Well. Does your sister still have it? Bill says then. Can we maybe get it back from her today?

No, no. I mean, she secretly took it but then she secretly brought it back. She put it back where it'd been, as if she'd never taken it. But when I looked inside it later I discovered she'd, uh. How to explain. She'd removed half, what she obviously thought was her half, of everything in it.

What, kept half the things? Bill says.

Yep.

What *was* in it?

Oh, just a lot of old sewing things, Patricia says.

Where's this case? Bill says. I don't remember ever seeing it. I don't remember it at all.

We don't have it any more, Patricia says. I threw it out.

Why? Bill says.

You know. I just didn't want it any more. So one day I bade it ceremonious farewell and I dumped it and all the things in it in the dustbin. Then the bin lorry came next day and took what was in the dustbin away. Gone forever.

Well, no, Bill says. Plasticized. That means it's probably still layered somewhere into landfill right now.

Like a meaningful meaningless time capsule, Patricia says.

And that case, Bill says, wherever it is, will basically outlast you *and* me *and* all the generations after us. Unless they ever do manage to develop a microbe that can eat all the plastics, it'll still be there in centuries' time, flattened under the surface of wherever it is like a new kind of sediment.

Oh God, Patricia says.

Then at some point in that future, Bill says, someone will find a way to make money out of that sediment. In which case –

In which case? Patricia says and smiles.

In which case the case of the stolen case will finally, at long last, be closed, Bill says.

A sedimental journey, Patricia says. There are some days, Billie Wild, especially days when I'm talking to you like this, it becomes clear as clearest air to me that family is never a closed case.

So, Bill says. Can I come? I mean – in case?

Patricia laughs.

She starts the ignition.

Because I don't know if I'm looking forward to having a sibling or not, Bill says.

They are driving down a road towards a sliproad towards the motorway.

Why are there all those flags up on the lampposts? Patricia says. Is it a holiday?

Where've you been? Bill says. Do you not live in the same country as I do? The one where some people have recently decided to use a flag that belongs to all of us as something to pressurize everybody about who gets to belong and who doesn't?

Oh God. Don't go getting any more political on me today, Bill, Patricia says. Enough on my school dinnerplate already.

Bill sighs, shields her eyes. Sunlight glances off the backs of the cars in front and blanks the windscreen; sunlit English uplands and downlands pass them at speed on either side.

What were you saying? Patricia says. Before the flag thing.

I was saying. I don't know if I want a sibling now if it's all envy over who gets what. If it involves people likely to steal into your house to, well, steal, and phonecalls late at night from people who sound like they might be a bit unstable.

Patricia laughs under her breath.

Let me explain, she says, what it's like having a sister. Even one who steals from you. So. Back when my mother died, as you know already, I took to sleeping in the shed. Not just sleeping in there but eating all my meals in there or out in the garden too, and only coming in to wash and to change my clothes when they needed changed. I didn't want to be in the house any more.

Why? Bill says.

I don't know. I just didn't. Anyway, me doing this made my father really angry at me. One day he demanded that I come back into the house. I refused. I was in the shed refusing through its door which I was holding just a crack open, enough for my nose, and I told him through the crack in it that I was never going to live in his house again and that nothing he could do could make me.

I watched him turn and walk halfway back up the garden. But then he turned round again and he ran at the door I was standing behind and he battered it open with his whole bodyweight.

I have a sense now that I shot backwards in the air, like someone in a cartoon. The door broke off its hinges. I fell quite hard under it against the bikes and the lawnmower.

He came into the shed, lifted the door off me and threw it to one side, picked me up, slung me under his arm, carried me into the house and dumped me down on the kitchen floor. He stood above me with one leg on either side of me like a colossus. I remember pressing myself into the linoleum like a miracle might let me pass right through it to escape.

What's a colossus? Bill says.

I don't know how to explain. A statue of a giant? Something colossal. He told me I belonged in this house and that I was to stay where I belonged. Then he told me to get up off the floor and make him a cup of tea and bring it out to him in the garden and that he was going out there now to get the pickaxe and the crowbar to take the roof off the shed so that there'd be no way anyone could sleep out there any more.

He went out, left the door open behind him. I heard him stamp off down the path. I waited flat on the kitchen floor for the noise of him demolishing the shed to start.

No noise.

I got up. I went and stood behind the open door and watched through the crack where the door hinge met the wood.

My sister, Petra, she'd have been twelve years old, that's all. A lot younger than you are now. Anyway she was standing down the garden in the doorway of the shed like she was there to stop him going into the shed. She had her arms folded. She was talking to him.

She finished talking to him, unfolded her arms and walked away from him back up the garden path. She came into the kitchen, winked at me and said,

it's fine now. You sleep out there for as long as you need to.

Here's what Patricia isn't saying out loud or even to herself about this story:

I see her framed in the broken open doorway of the shed.

I see her incline her head towards those toys our uncle brought us, matted and filthy on the compost heap.

She is saying calm as anything,

helpless looking things. Little talking toys. Anyone can press a button on them to hear them say the rubbish they've been programmed to say. We are not them. We are nobody's toys. We are not just something that can belong to anyone else, a condolence present, a stupid inanimate product from a shop. Do not treat us as if we are. Believe me, we will not speak rubbish. We will speak the truth. And just because it looks like she's gone doesn't mean she's gone. She is speaking to you right now through me. All of which means my little sister can do what she likes. And that you'll let her. If she wants to sleep in the shed, she gets to sleep in the shed. It won't be for long. She just needs time. She'll come back into the house by herself when she chooses to. But if you don't let her do what she needs to do now, or you hurt her because of it, or you bully her, or me, even just one more time, even just a little, I will start speaking truth really loud. I will tell everybody you know about how you hurt our mother. Don't think I won't. Don't think I don't know. I might look like nothing to you but I am very powerful. I know everything. You know they all know already. You know they're just waiting for us to let them know we know so someone can do something about it. Don't you raise your hand at me. Put your arm down. Good. Right. Now. Here's the deal. I will not trouble you provided you don't trouble her and you don't trouble me.

 I see him raise himself up at the shoulders again as if to hit her. I see her not flinch, not move an inch, wait to see if he's going to dare to.

 I see the moment pass. His shoulders fall. His arms come down to his sides.

 All the years later I am still asking myself.

 Did my father hurt my mother?

 He must've at the very least thought or believed he did, to respond like that.

Did people know something about us I didn't know?
Did I myself know something I didn't know?
Did I choose not to see it?
Why would I do that?
There she is, look, standing in front of him in the broken doorway.
Now go to the garden centre and buy some new hinges and put this door back on the shed so she can sleep in here again tonight, should she choose to, my sister says.

Wow. She sorted it, Bill is saying meanwhile next to her in the car. How did she do that? Did it work?

For quite a while, Patricia says. Yes. It did. I was in awe, too, for quite a while. I'd see her and I'd think, oh my God. That person is my sister. But that's enough about the distant past. Let's use this time together now that you're trapped here next to me with nowhere else to go to talk about why you don't go to school enough.

Bill holds up her phone.

This is all the education I need, she says.

That's what I'm worried about, Patricia says.

Yeah, but don't worry. I'm not stupid, Bill says.

That's the thing about education and school, Patricia says. It's how people commonly get to be the opposite of stupid. That's how come you're *not* stupid, because you're actively getting an education.

I don't think school's the same nowadays as it was back in your day, Bill says.

Ah yes, back in Victorian England, Patricia says. When we all wore costume drama clothes to school. I can't imagine it'll be *that* much different now than it was then. Apart from the getting to wear pretty much what you like to school all the time. That's definitely different.

Did boys and some girls in your classes bark at the female teachers in the classroom in the middle of the lessons in those days long ago when you were at school? Bill says.

Do what?

Like a pack of dogs? To let her know they think she's a bitch?

Well, the teachers they're barking at can't be much good as teachers, if they're letting that kind of thing happen in a class, Patricia says.

See? You know nothing, Bill says. Did boys in your classes shout stuff all the time, in class and out of it, about girls and women being naturally subservient?

No. Back in the liberated wild and free 1990s, Patricia says, we were just supposed to accept that though we all believed we were completely freed up and dehistoricized, actually we were still meant to be subservient after all and to just accept it and get on with it. But at least we had birth control, and people used condoms, and we talked a lot about how much more free we were. Things could've been worse.

They soooo aaaaare, Bill says in a horror film way.

And you're at the best school in the district, Patricia says. By far.

I know, Bill says. Why do you think I *do* still go into school for some of the classes? Anyway I'm going to need qualifications.

Qualifications for what?

Journalism.

Journalism?

Bill waits, says nothing.

Journalism! Patricia says. Okay. That's great. That's wonderful. Yes. Good for you. What kind of journalism?

Long form investigative, Bill says.

Can people study that? Specifically?

I don't know yet, Bill says. I think it might just mean it's journalism that's investigative and long. Anyway. It's the kind I've decided I'm going to do.

When did you decide this?

Recently, Bill says. So. Don't worry about me and school.

Okay, Patricia says. But. To go to journalism school you'll definitely need to pass some exams.

Yeah. I've looked into it. I'm on it. I know what I'll need.

And also. I'll need to find a new job, Patricia says.

I'll work out a way to fund it, Bill says. No worries.

We'll both work it out, Patricia says.

Will we? Bill says.

We'll do it, Patricia says. We'll make it work. Why did you decide this?

I just did, Bill says. No reason. Tell me some stuff from the lovely innocent past when people could go to college and get tertiary educated even though they had no money.

I'm afraid I missed out on those hazy days myself, Patricia says.

Tell me more stuff about what it's like having a sister, Bill says. Now that I know you have one. And that I'll maybe have one soon.

I know. That's so great. Isn't it? Patricia says. It'll be great.

Or a brother, Bill says. Have you got a secret possible brother as well hidden away somewhere?

Nope. No brother, Patricia says. Just Petra. My mother had a brother but we only met him after she died. He came to my mother's funeral. Nobody spoke to him at all. He sat on his own at the back of the crematorium and wandered about by himself in the house afterwards. My father and his friends all did this tacit ignoring. Nobody even said hello to him.

Except you. And your sister, obvs, Bill says. What were you both like when you were my age?

I was exactly the same as I am now. Obvs.

Yeah. Right.

But Petra, when she was your age, Patricia says. She started wearing these ostentatiously unfashionable clothes. She looked great. She looked like she was a Romany boy in a children's story. Neighbours began to treat her as if she was a bit dangerous, or mad, or maybe taking drugs because of it. Maybe she was. She would skip down our staircase with the light glinting off these shiny things and places in her clothes, sewn in little mirrors and so on, as graceful and as bright as, as, I don't know, as the light falling through the glass panel in the front door at the foot of the stairs, the way it fell on the plastic matting my father put down on the hall carpet to keep it good.

Lot of plastic in that house you grew up in, Bill says.

I felt like a shadow, compared to her, Patricia says. I didn't mind. I liked it. I liked the idea that if I was her shadow it meant we were definitely joined forever to each other. And, of course, I was also a bit envious. And fiercely determined to be better than her.

At what?

At everything, Patricia says. At, just, you know, being. I was very competitive. But there was no point. Petra was paramount.

What, like the streaming channel?

Ha ha. Yes! Living with her *was* a bit like constant streaming, a never ending box set, episode after episode, The Petra Show. Exactly like living with that small screen grandeur of the little film clip of the mountain with the clouds floating past it that they used to show on TV at the start of every Popeye cartoon or Paramount film.

What-eye cartoon? Bill says.

Popeye, Patricia says. Eats spinach out of tins he squeezes open with his fist. Beats people up. I haven't seen a Popeye cartoon for years, they're not around any more. I presume because they're all about beating people up. But they taught people a bit about nutrition, at least.

Then Patricia says something Bill can't quite hear because they're on the motorway now.

Patricia presses the buttons and the windows go up.

Did I really just hear you say, Bill says, that your sister could *talk to the dead*?

She could, you know.

Bit of a one way conversation, Bill says.

That's not my experience of your possible aunt Petra, Patricia says.

What's that mean?

Nothing you'd understand. Unless you'd grown up with her.

Like how?

Well, Patricia says.

Was she, like, a medium? Bill says.

A social medium, Patricia says. Ha ha. No, what she did was, she could take something dead or even someone dead, I don't mean our parents or anyone real, anyone we knew, nothing like that. I mean an anonymous someone you'd no way of knowing about, someone no one had any way of really knowing anything about any more. Or she could take something that was a dead weight in you, I mean in me, and she could give it a story, a voice. And then that dead thing stopped being a dead weight, it came alive, and because it did it started to carry itself. After that, whatever it was didn't seem so hopeless any more.

?? Bill says without saying anything.

I can't explain, Patricia says. I can't say more than that she could take something crushed and ruined and she'd make up something about it and it would give it back to itself. Still ruined. But also weirdly sort of *un*ruined.

By making things up? Bill says.

She was exceptionally good at making things up, Patricia says.

About dead people? Bill says. You said she made up someone dead.

As I said, not somebody we personally knew, Patricia says.

So, you made up lies about someone you didn't know? Bill says.

Well, when we were quite small, Patricia says.

We made up a ghost. I pretended I could see him, though I couldn't, I couldn't see anything, and she pretended she could hear him, and she was very convincing. She made up a whole story about him. We called him Glyph.

Gliff? Like that book I read last month?

Different spelling. Glyph like in hieroglyph, or petroglyph.

Oh, Bill says. Like the word at the start of the weedkiller?

What weedkiller? Patricia says.

The one that's in soil and water and most foods and in wine and in beer. I don't know how to pronounce it, Bill says.

She spells it:

GLYPHOSATE

Not a word I know, Patricia says. Not something I've ever heard of.

It's heard of you, Bill says. It's heard of me too. It's in us right now. It's bad for bees and worms and birds and fish and possibly bigger creatures too, like cats, and the councils all over the country use it to kill the weeds on roads in towns and cities so it's ubiquitous. As far as humans go it's labelled *probably carcinogenic*, which probably means it is. But the companies that sell it don't want people to think it is, so they come down heavily on anything that suggests it is, and for some reason the government here keeps saying they'll ban it but pushing back the date when it'll be banned. Every year they push it back another year. As if it's not already all through the substrata anyway.

Through the what? Patricia says.

The substrata.

Oh. How do you know any of this? Patricia says.

We all should, Bill says. I can't believe you don't. It's happening to us all and it's so unsaid. I am definitely going to write about it one day.

Long form? Patricia says. Investigative?

I'll write it on every wall, Bill says. Why did you name your ghost this word? And how, anyway, did you ever bring some random dead person back to life, did you do new age spells with burning sage and set things on fire and dance round them? Or is this person we're going to meet today more like an AI avatar?

Ha. No, Patricia says. The polar opposite. And I see what you're saying, but it's very different. Because AI doesn't really bring people back from the dead.

Yes it does.

But not really, Patricia says. They're not really there. It's a machine projection.

And your sister *really did* bring back someone from the dead? Bill says.

Well, no, not exactly. More imaginatively than actually.

So. Same as AI.

No. It's different, Patricia says.
How?
Bill. Don't get me started on AI, Patricia says.
I wouldn't dare, Bill says.
Because being a person will always involve metaphysics whether we know it or not, Patricia says.
Here we go, Bill says.
And AI has no metaphysics, Patricia says. It might 'know' about metaphysics. It can be told about metaphysics. But a machine will never have a metaphysic. It has no mystery.
Who says it doesn't have metaphysics? Bill says. How do you know? AI can do it all *and* have it all.
AI *will* have it all, Patricia says. If we're not careful. And do you even know what metaphysics means?
You're just annoyed at AI because you lost your job, Bill says.
Yes, Patricia says. I am. You're right. I'm aggrieved. But not because I lost my job. More because when machines start being the arbiters, for humans, of what being human is, then I want to be there to check that all the things, all the possibilities of what it means to be human, are somewhere in that mix. Because every person has a soul. And no machine ever will.
I'll just point out that the last statement you made doesn't logically follow on from what you were saying before it, Bill says. And I have my own

theories about machines, actually, and people's extended use of them. Souls, I've no theories on. Except that I'm not sure they exist.

Ah well. You're young yet, Patricia says.

Patronize much? Bill says. But AI. Really. Patricia. It really helps people. Jenna at school's uncle has leukaemia and AI found more than a hundred other people in Europe his blood could be exactly matched to for stem cell transplant. At the press of a key. A few seconds. In the old days it apparently took months. And there's that news story about the woman who died, who had a disease that meant she stopped being able to speak in a way that anyone could understand, and how AI took a tape of her saying something decades ago that sounded like nothing but fuzz and cleaned it up and reanimated her voice so that her daughter, who had never heard her mother's voice before, could hear it for the first time.

That's more what I'd call intelligent use of tech, Patricia says.

She laughs a sad laugh.

Listen to me. No, I mean, don't listen to me.

Which? Bill says.

I'm an ancient fragment. Happy to be a broken piece of something. Sad to be it too. I think I'm what used to be called a flat character.

What's a flat character? Bill says. Something in coding?

Ha. No, Patricia says. It's way older than that. It's from back when I studied books, and literature, and their devices. It means someone in a book, a character, who has no arc of a story and no development of self. No complexity. A shadow. Yep, don't listen to me. I'm a shadow.

The thing is, Patricia, I myself see you as very substantial, Bill says.

Thank you, Patricia says. I appreciate your support. Unless that's you telling me I need to lose weight.

No, because if I was going to tell you that, Bill says, what I'd do is I'd send it anonymously to all your social media threads and try to ignite a pile on of messages about your appearance so as to let you know what's acceptable and what isn't.

Tch. Got to learn. Got to get it right, Patricia says.

If you're ever going to get down with the kids at school, Bill says.

Here's what the flat character / literary device called Patricia is thinking about after that conversation, with equally literary device but maybe slightly less flat character Bill asleep now next to her in the passenger seat as they head towards London.

Soul clap your hands. No. Something more impersonal. Clap its hands.

A Yeats poem? A person is a tattered coat on a stick unless their soul claps its hands and sings, then sings even louder. The actual line is miles better than this. I'll look it up when we get to wherever it is we're going. (I have a sister and I've never even seen the flat she lives in yet. Is that weird?) *How would a soul sing? What would it sing? What would it sound like?* Remember that lecturer saying this, young and beardy, long hair.

We found out years later he had a habit of choosing a different student from final year to sleep with every year. That can't have been easy, for girl after girl, for all the years. Not me, thank God. Though, would I have said yes and gone for it, flattered, fucked over, if it had been me? Probably.

Does a soul have hands? <u>Can</u> it applaud? he said. We wrote it down. I did, anyway. He told us, soulful chap, that when he was a child he'd imagined the soul as a sort of purified lozenge shaped thing with no eyes, no mouth, no features at all, a bit medicinal like a cough sweet. We all laughed. He told us about Hadrian when he was dying, writing the truly lovely little poem to his soul. Animula, vagula, blandula. *Gentle little wanderer, my soul. My guest and my soul mate, here in my body. Where are you heading now? Somewhere bare, somewhere there'll be no more jokes between us.*

I wrote it down on the foolscap page, I remember it there in the margin, in my writing. He told us about St Augustine and the body being the horse and the soul its rider and that the two couldn't be parted or that'd be the journey over. Then he sent us all off to find the story of Nietzsche crossing the road in a city one winter day to put his arms around the neck of a horse which a coachman or merchant has been beating so hard that its legs have given way and it's lying on the ground.

The story is probably apocryphal. It's meant to

be about Nietzsche losing his mind. At the end of that story he's demented, never speaks out loud again.

For me, though. Here's the moment a soul meant I heard the real rhythm of things:

I was told the child was a possible. She was three years old, nearly four. This was the first meeting, in the garden of the institutional place. I'd been briefed and screened over and over by the psychologists. Then I'd been given the full file to read.

The child had been left on her own in a roomful of people all unconscious because of whatever shit they'd taken. She had known to phone for an ambulance when she couldn't waken her mother.

That detail. I knew something about that.

When the ambulance got to the place, the report said, the child had been found wrapped in a jacket on the floor. This was because, as the child told the ambulance team, while all the people were sleeping she had been picking up pieces of glass off the floor and taking them one by one over to the rubbish pile by the bin in the kitchen so that nobody else would step on it and hurt themselves. Then when she'd seen that her feet had started bleeding and that she was making a mess of the carpet she'd sat down and tucked her feet into the jacket, one foot in each sleeve, so she wouldn't make any more mess.

When they offered her a biscuit in the hospital

she told them, it said in the file, that she had eaten something she found in the rubbish pile and that it had tasted very nice.

I was not at all sure I'd be able to handle a child who'd already seen so much. I feared my own childishness.

When I came into the garden you were lying barefoot on your front on a little grassy mound. You were examining a patch of lawn daisies there in the grass you were lying in.

I sat down on the mound next to you.

Hello, I said.

Hello, you said without looking up.

Are you Billie? I said.

Yes, you said.

I'm Patricia, I said. Will we pick some of the flowers? We can make a necklace for you if we do.

Oh no, you said. It would be a shame. I don't need a necklace thank you.

You looked at me for a moment. Then you sat up cross legged holding your feet in your hands. I saw the lines of scars on the healed places in the soles of your feet.

Actual pain went through me, followed by sadness.

Both these things had some other something beyond them. Surety? Acceptance?

Calm.

That's the moment I committed fully.

You answered some questions. You asked me about the picture of a dog on my T-shirt. What is the dog's name? you said.

It doesn't have a name yet, I said. You can give it its name if you like.

You nodded, noncommittal. But what you really wanted to do was to lie down with your head among the flowers again.

On those flowers, you said, on the petals of that one there, there is the little bit of pink in the very ends. It is nearly invisible but it is there.

Invisible? I said surprised at a small child knowing the word.

It means you can't see it. But it is nearly invisible, not invisible.

Let's see, I said.

I got down to eye level with you. So close to them the flowers were as big as me. One was pink tipped, closed. The next was open, bright white and yellow. Its yellow eye looked like it was made of hundreds of tiny yellow shrubs the size of goose pimples on skin.

Some of the flowers were tattered and done. Others were as if proclaiming their name. Daisies!

Every one of them was pushing away from the ground, reaching up out of itself to another source.

Let's shift from Patricia's perspective over to Bill's now in this story, because the woman who answers the door of the flat in the little block they park outside looks so like Patricia – but so isn't in any other way remotely like Patricia – that Bill is shocked speechless at seeing both these things at once in a stranger.

A memory kicks off in Bill's head. All the other times she's had this memory she's believed it to be the memory of a dream, one where she is very small and there are two Patricias, one on either side of her, and they are swinging her with one of her hands in each of theirs up in the air and down again as they all walk to the shops together.

Wild Bill Hiccup.

Hi, Patricia says. This is Billie. Remember Billie?

That's not Billie, the woman says. Where's the

small child gone that you had with you the last time I saw you?

Don't ask me, Patricia says.

I'm Bill, Bill says.

Take your word for it, the woman says.

You look the same, though, Patricia says. How the hell are you pulling that off?

You do too, Patch, the woman says. Come in.

The woman shows them into the lounge space. She keeps saying the word patch. Patch patch patch. It is the name she calls Patricia.

Thank you both for coming, the woman says. Have a seat, Billie. I'd say sit down Patch but I just need your eye on something right away, right now.

Right now? Patricia says. Okay.

Bill sits on the edge of a sofa next to a rolled up sleeping bag while the woman who resembles Patricia takes Patricia through and across the hall. Then the woman comes back and stands in the doorway of the lounge and waits while Patricia opens a door somewhere Bill can't see.

And you want me to help clear it up, is that it? Patricia says.

The woman says something Bill can't hear.

Hoarse? Patricia says. Nope.

Okay. Wait. I'm coming, the woman says.

She crosses the hall. Bill hears her say, scone.

Hoarse? Patricia says.

Oh man, the woman says like she's shaking her head.

A man as well? Patricia says.

No. Just a little hoarse.

Or no. It's the word *horse* she's saying.

Petra, Patricia says. You been taking horse?

They both laugh, like drugs are a joke.

Absolutely nothing, the woman says. Thank God.

So uh horse did this, and now there's no horse? Patricia says.

Swear to heaven. Went in there last night. It was there.

Then they start talking about a blind.

Bill can't hear well enough. She gets up off the sofa and comes through. The bedroom is like it's been ransacked. People off their heads on something must have broken in here and done this. There are clothes and books thrown all over the floor. A big heavy looking bookcase is on its side; the furniture is all over the place and some of it is wrecked. There's a desk with a broken leg. A wardrobe door is hanging off. The bed is shoved up against other furniture. Bedding is flung everywhere.

Bill's seen worse.

Were you robbed? she says to the woman.

The woman shakes her head.

No, she says.

I was explaining to Billie you can sometimes be a bit imaginative, Patricia says.

Never anywhere near as powerfully imaginative as Patch, though, the woman says.

Not a patch on Patch! Confirmation at last, Patricia says.

She stands and claps her hands like a child. It is a bit bewildering. It is like Patricia has changed into a different person now that she's here.

Patch is the one who could always see, the woman is saying to Bill. I could never see anything. I thought, if there's anything here to see, then Patch'll see it. When we were kids. She could.

The woman, Petra, looks traumatized. She has black rings round her eyes like she hasn't slept for a week.

No, Patricia says. I never really saw anything. It was all made up.

Then she winks. It's not clear whether it's Bill she's winking at or it's the woman. They are clearly playing some psychohysterical family game that has its own rules and language.

But Bill is used to what family can do to people. When family happens, at whatever level, you have to wait it out. There's nothing else you can do. So she is philosophical about it.

She looks at Patricia and the woman, each a real person accompanied by something a bit like a mirror image.

Uh huh, Bill says, whatever. But whatever you two are on, and whatever's gone down here, someone'll need to open a window in this flat soon. It really smells of horseshit in here.

Both Patricia and the woman turn at the same time at the same speed and look at Bill when she says this. They stare at her like they've seen a ghost.

What? Bill says.

Bill has finally worked out that apparently a 'ghost horse' from a story about some people in the First World War 'did this' to Patricia's sister's room. But the beaten up bedroom has been straightened out and put right. The bed has been remade with clean linen. The things that were everywhere on the floor are all put away. The bookcase is back up against a wall, the books back on it in alphabetical order; Petra has rubbish taste. Almost no fiction. No poetry. Just books about people who made bridges, historical biographies, books about the industrial revolution, mining, books about ancient archaeological finds in English caves, a book about the history of skiing, books about kinds of field grasses, the history of concrete, how people lived in the 1920s and 1930s. The endless history of history. The broken furniture is now out of the flat and on top of a lot of waste stuff in a skip a builder is using for a renovation job a couple of blocks down; Bill carried it round and shoved it in under the tarpaulin without anyone stopping her or objecting.

As she went down the road carrying the broken chair she was shaking her head to herself.

Patricia's sister Petra thinks she's being haunted by a fucking *horse*?

Okay. Petra is crazy.

But Patricia is also acting a little crazy, like it's contagious. Or maybe this is a sisterly thing, a thing that happens when you've got a sister, and she's doing it to keep her sister company.

Bill has seen madnesses move through people before. She is careful to allow it.

Now she is sitting in the lounge place again. It is pretty horrible in here, not like anyone's home in any way. It is a bit like a very standard Airbnb. A TV. A table. An armchair. A sofa. It is a bit like someone lives here who never lives here or has anything to do with anyone else.

She breathes in deep, out through her mouth.

This is a useful skill. It slows things.

Patricia is in the kitchen part of the room, where she has found enough in Petra's fridge to make something that will go with pasta. Petra comes and sits beside Bill on the sofa while Patricia fills pans with water and cuts olives into small pieces.

Why do you call her Patch? she asks Petra.
Petra looks at Bill like she'll maybe kill her.
Because it's her name, Petra says.
Patch is what my mother called me, Patricia calls across the room. She was Petra. So I was Patch. From Blue Peter.
She said we were her loyal pack, Petra says.
Her loyal pack of TV dogs, Patricia says. Apparently they had dogs called these names on Blue Peter when my mother was a small child.
Awkward silence.
Bill clears her throat.
Did you ever, Petra, when *I* was small, call me the name Wild Bill Hiccup?
Oh God. Maybe. I don't know, Petra says. Probably.
She nods towards the kitchen island.
It sounds more like her thing, though, she says. Given the punning and all.
Petra takes a box of tobacco off a table and starts fiddling with cigarette papers.
You know smoking's really bad for you and for anybody else who breathes in the smoke from your smoking? Bill says.
Gosh, Billie. I didn't immediately take you for a moralizing disciplinarian, Petra says.
Proven fact, Bill says.
Proven fact too that it's my house, no? Petra says.

But she puts down the papers, puts down the box with a little slam on the table.

Well, no. The bank's house, she says.

She laughs to herself.

Awkward silence again.

I'm sorry, Petra says. I'm not much good with kids.

That's okay because I'm now old enough to get married, to have to join the military should they ever decide to conscript us, and if there's another general election by chance quite soon to vote in it, Bill says.

Ah. Sorry, Petra says. Sorry, Billie. Point taken. And thanks. Really. For helping clear up the room.

No problem, Bill says.

She sees a book open with its pages flat to the floor under the armchair on the other side of the room.

I've read that book, she says. The book about the kids with the horse.

Oh yeah, Petra says. Patch sent it to me.

She fishes it out from under the chair. She tries to close it but it's a paperback and the fact that it's been lying open on the floor makes it hard to close it without it springing back open by itself so she puts it down closed on the table and puts an empty coffee pot on top of it to keep it shut.

I found it a little blatant, Petra says. I was left

quite uneasy by it. But then. I don't read much fiction any more.

Silence.

Can I ask you something? Bill says.

I don't know, Petra says. Can you?

Then she winks at Bill.

Do you think you saw a horse in your room because you'd been reading about one in that book? Bill says.

Petra makes a face, shakes her head.

Longer silence.

Did you really see a horse? Bill says. A real horse?

Petra shrugs.

I'd been looking up history, trying to verify an old family story, she says. I think I may've just lost it for a bit. My mind, I mean. But yes. I did. I saw a blind horse. In my bedroom. I heard it first, then I saw it. It was real. It was warm to the touch. It was breathing. It had a wet nose, I saw its nostrils literally glisten. I saw it as clear and as here as I'm seeing you now. So. Are you here or not?

I'm as here as you are, Bill says. What made you think it was blind?

Petra shrugs again.

I've never seen a blind horse, she says. I don't know what they're supposed to look like. I've hardly ever seen any horse so close up. But its eyes were white, like milky white lids had formed on top of them. It was awful, an awful thing to see. I also saw its whiskers round its mouth, its, muzzle I think the word is. See? I don't even know the word for it. I don't know the first thing about horses. I don't think I even knew till now that they *have* these, sort of, whiskery hairs round their mouths. Well, this one did and its mouth was sort of soft. It was a darker grey round its mouth than its nose.

Silence.

The worst thing is, she says. It was scared. And I didn't know how to help it. So I sat on the bed for a bit, just sat with it in the room. Then I put a pan full of water in there and I just shut the door on it, I didn't go back in. I stayed in here all night. I didn't open the door. The first time I looked in there again is now. When you arrived.

And it's not there now, Bill says.

What's that poem about the man on the stair who wasn't there? Patricia says. Something something on the stair, I met a man who wasn't there. He wasn't there again today. Oh how I wish he'd go away.

Comforting, Petra says. Not.

Bill sees that Petra's hand is shaking.

Petra sees her see it.

It wouldn't be shaking if I'd had a cigarette, she says. It's your fault it's shaking. Not some made up horse's fault.

One of my friends' mothers has a horse, Bill says. I mean a real one. They rent a field on a farm for it.

Silence.

It's apparently quite expensive, to keep a horse, Bill says.

Great, Petra says. What about a horse apparition? What's the cost of those?

If wishes were horses, Patricia calls. Then beggars something.

Beggars belief, Petra says.

Silence. Awkward. Patricia knocks pans about in the kitchen. Steam comes off boiling water. Petra coughs.

Excuse me, she says. I haven't had much sleep. As you might imagine.

Patricia says you know about ears, noses and throats, Bill says.

A bit, Petra says. Ears, mostly.

It's particularly vocal cords I'm interested in, Bill says. Do you know anything about vocal cords?

Not much. But everything's connected, Petra says. The eustachian tube goes between the inner ear and the throat. So I know a little bit, yes.

What happens if you take someone's vocal cords out? Bill says.

What a question. What, remove them? You mean if somebody's ill or something?

Could someone still make a noise if their vocal cords were gone? Bill says.

Well, I assume what'd happen would be just what you'd imagine, Petra says. No more naturally being able to project sound. But you *would* still be able to whisper, you just need air for that. So language itself wouldn't completely stop for a person with no vocal cords. And there are many other ways to communicate. There's voice prosthesis.

What's that? Bill says.

Like having a prosthetic limb. You know. Like if you lose a leg or a hand they can give you pretty good replacements now that can do things legs or hands can do, and they can do something similar for gone vocal cords too, a sort of valve they put in the throat. There's also a little machine you can put against your neck and speak through. It works by vibration. But honestly? I don't know much about it. Mostly I deal with people with tinnitus.

Is that a disease? Bill says.

No. It's more a symptom.

Of what?

Ah. That's the question, Petra says. Tinnitus is mysterious. People who've got tinnitus can hear all sorts of sounds that don't exist at all externally.

They hear things that don't exist? Bill says.

No. They *do* exist, the sounds, they really do, but can only be heard by the person who's got the tinnitus. Nothing and no one else can trace them or hear them or record them. Not yet anyway. That's the pot of gold at the end of contemporary tinnitus research.

But if it can't be proved they exist, why does anyone believe the people who say the noises exist? Bill says.

I can't answer that, Petra says. All I'll say is, you're young. And you're tinnitus free. So in the course of the coming years don't turn your headphones or your earbuds up too loud. Or hit your head against any brick walls. Nobody knows for sure what causes it, but probably damage of some sort. Age damage. Too much noise. Injury maybe, trauma, whiplash. Could be chemical substances. Certain antidepressants. Or it could just be blood vessels or muscles expanding and contracting. It could be noise in the eustachian tube, or the nervous system registering abnormal auditories.

Okay, Bill says. Got it. Thanks for telling me.

And they're starting to think it might be a natural fight-or-flight response to even an exceptionally mild level of hearing loss, Petra says. As if the brain of the person who's got even a tiny bit of hearing loss worries about it so much that it, the brain I mean, starts testing the person's hearing all the time to make sure that person can still hear – and it does this by quite literally making up sounds, on purpose, invented by the brain and nothing else, to see if the person can hear them.

The brain makes up sounds? Imaginary sounds? What kind of sounds? Patricia shouts over from the kitchen area.

Oh God. All sorts. Buzzing. Hissing. Whistling. High pitched. Low pitched. Some people hear a roaring noise, or what sounds like bagpipe tunes or klezmer. Some hear what they call a kind of white noise. Some think it sounds like a desk fan that's been left on, or a plane that's eternally taking off, an eternal engine. Some people hear what sounds like fish frying, or water constantly running. Some people hear a pulsing noise. Like their hearts are in their ears.

And you test them and you really truly never hear any of the things they say they can hear? Patricia says.

My job's very minor, Petra says. I do an initial assessment of their hearing levels and pass on the results. That's all I do.

Patricia comes through and sits on the arm of the sofa.

Does it mean, then, that the people who have it can't hear properly over the top of it? she says.

No. More often than not they can hear perfectly well over it, or through it. But tinnitus can be depressing. It can drive people insane. In the old days people trepanned the people who said they had it, to release through the holes they made in their skulls whatever creature or spirit might be living in their heads making the noise. As you might imagine, that didn't work. The egyptians thought the ears of people who had it had been enchanted by dark magic. They used frankincense. That didn't work either.

What does work? Patricia says.

Sympathy. CBT. That's therapy.

We know what therapy is, Bill says. We have meetings with Kayleigh, don't we?

But now Patricia is saying something to her sister and her sister is saying something back.

– tell them they can learn to live with it, she is saying. Psychological encouragement. Positivity. Sometimes we do scans, especially if the tinnitus is one sided, to check everything's okay with the brain. But yeah. It can ruin a life. The fear of the unknown.

What about the fear of the known? Bill says. Can that ruin a life?

Neither Patricia nor Petra seems to hear her.

I always tell the people I see who have it diagnosed, Petra says, about all the famous people who have it or have had it. Barbra Streisand has it.

All that singing, Patricia says.

Goya had it.

All that war, Patricia says.

Van Gogh.

Why he cut off that ear I presume, Patricia says.

Jonathan Swift.

Why he invented Gulliver the giant with a townful of tiny people squeaking at his ears, Patricia says.

Best of all. Beethoven.

Maker-up of sublime sounds, Patricia says.

And, well, worst of all. Hitler.

All that declamatory poison going in at the ear.

Like with Hamlet's father? Bill says.

Hergé's Adventures of Tintinnabulation! Patricia says in a pretend thriller voice over the top of Bill speaking.

Petra laughs.

But God, Patricia says. Bells ringing in your head all the time. Imagine. You'd be on constant alert. Alarm! War! War's over! Invasion! Liberation! Celebration! Transubstantiation!

What's transubstantiation? Bill says.

They don't hear her. It's like they themselves have been enchanted. Or are just enchanted with each other.

She's a sixteen year old nobody in the room.

Well.

Family almost always means someone somewhere doesn't get to be it.

All just so much somatosound, Petra is saying. All in a day's work.

You say somato, Patricia says. And I say somayto.

Laughter.

Bill sinks back into the couch and into herself.

She centres herself on the place in her throat. She hums to herself a little to feel the exact presence in her. True vocal folds. False vocal folds. Vestibular folds. Inner lining of trachea. Epiglottis. Glottis.

These are how anything gets said out loud, whether it gets heard or it doesn't.

Bill Wild leaves them to it. Whatever *it* is.

She goes outside and sits on the little wall at the front of the block of flats.

She DMs Jenna:

squirrels in the attic alert! frenzy alert! trigger warning alert! pattericiana has taken me to meet relative of hers who talks about kind of people who *hear sounds no one else can hear but them* that *only exist in their heads nowhere else* & this person has a visitation from a get this Jen deep breath ready? spirit phantom apparition wraith shade spook spectre ghoul scooby-dooby-whooo-hooOOoooey H O R S E that is a GHOST she says this horse/ghost GHORST went ballistic in her bedroom & told me she could 'see its whiskers' (another shot of whisk(er)y anyone?) I am not makin this up you couldn make it up

psycho case or what? she says its historic & is
TRIGGER WARNING UPSETTING SCENES
a BLIND HORSE FROM 100 YEARS AGO
lost its eyes in the anthem for doomed youth
trenches & has decided to come & live at hers
now for foreseeable or praps she means the not
seeable. I myself have not yet seen it hahaha but
pattericiana in her patterician way is takin it
seriously well its her family eh bred in the bones
but not my bones thank fuck & the woman does
look spooked. Think the world is gettin to them
def gettin to me how was PE how was maths
how was Eng I am in the mind forged maniacal
London with the chimney sweepers cry ghostin
me & can <u>you</u> hear the squirrels? oh nooo
TRIGGER WARNING PSYCHOLOGICAL
ANGST am I the <u>only person in the world who
can hear</u> the squirrels of madderness I am tellin
you now they are chewin on my electrics. Can
you see the blind horse? me I cant but I tell you
if I do see a horse any horse at all I will get on its
back & canter it far far away from here ghorst
or no.

    She has to do a double DM because she runs out
of characters halfway through.

    She sits on the wall and looks round at the
neighbourhood.

    There is no place less likely for a horse, dead or
alive, to want to come to, to be honest.

She thinks of the field Jenna's mother's horse is in. Lush, open, green as if forever.

But there is a drying green down the side of the block where it could eat something, if ghost horses need to eat, and a square of grass in front of it that's been wired off with a sign she can read from here saying:

! Warning !
Dangerous site
Children must not play on this site!
No Ball Games
No Unauthorized Entry

They could break down that fence if they need to. It's not very substantial.

When she looks at her phone again she sees that Jenna has sent her back this.

It is film footage 1 min 43 seconds long from one of the wars happening now, probably Gaza because of the backdrop of miles of grey ruin behind it.

The film is of a pile of bricks and stones.

Nothing happens.

Then the broken bricks and chunks of building start to move and heave, back and fore, like they're breathing.

A horse's head, the bridge of the nose first, pushes through and out of the pile of stuff and thrashes around.

It is a horsehead made of dust.

Dust and rubbly shapes shake loose down from the ears and off the neck. Front legs are suddenly there and scrabbling, and a broad chest appears, back legs appear, kicking and finding their footing, then the whole brickheap rises like it's getting to its feet itself, as the horse does, as the horse sheds the broken stuff. Then a horse the colour of stonedust and concrete stands in a spill of broken stones and concrete, dust rising off it like smoke. It shakes itself out of there and stumbles over the stones and away.

Next Jenna sends her a message and a photo.

The message says this:

There was once a famous horse called Trigger. Trigger Warning good name for racehorse we will one day win the National with Bill also my phone just sent me this other memory do you remember Mr Martino in Eng said we had to write about what if you could bring some random person from history the past etc back to life who would it be + why + you wrote down this + I took this photo

The photo is of the page of a jotter, and written on it in Bill's handwriting:

I would not want to bring anybody back, it would be like Frankenstein and the monster to do this. But if someone from history that I would choose to bring back to life did arrive back in life then this person would be saying something like this – 'I am here because I was here and I've come back because when I was here there was one day I stood under an old plum tree with my friend and blossom fell from it all around us like warm snow.'

Bill is now standing outside the lounge door and listening to them inside holding forth. They are arguing about something. It sounds like they're saying the word thimble. The argument sounds real. Then it dissolves into laughing. They continue to exclaim about thimbles for a while.

It soon becomes apparent that they're several bottles down.

Bill hates it when Patricia drinks.

She can't help hating it. It is like watching someone become a deformed version of themselves, like something that had a shape has blurred its shape and thinks it's really great to do that.

(nota bene note it well Bill the *moralizing disciplinarian*.)

Then they are talking about a man who is something to do with Patricia. Apparently Patricia sees this man from time to time. He still can't talk to her but he watches TV with her.

Eventually Bill realizes that it's not a real man they're talking about but someone they made up, the friendly ghost with the weedkiller name Patricia told her about in the car.

She gathers that Patricia sometimes still likes to imagine she's watching Four in a Bed with him.

Did she really just hear Patricia say that this ghost especially enjoys the older episodes where the film quality is a bit bleached out? That he's relaxed and happy when all the people on it are nice to each other? That he silently frets a lot when the people on it fight with each other and are unpleasant about the amounts they have or haven't paid for their overnight bed and breakfast stay?

– tethered to this for life too? Petra is saying. Because last night was terrifying. I'm terrified. I don't think I can do this. Not longterm.

I don't look on it as tethered, Patricia is saying. I look on it more as hospitality. In your case, horspitality.

Don't, Petra says. Not funny. And why is it the *horse* that turns up? Not that poor boy they shot. I can tell what the boy turning up might be asking, or even in need of. But what's a horse going to want of *me*?

I can't answer that, Patricia says, not being a horse myself.

That's it. No joke. Bill's heard enough.
She turns a full circle in the hall.
But there's nowhere for her to go.
She pushes the door and comes into the room.
It smells of cigarettes in here. She sits on the couch next to Patricia. She puts the heels of her hands into her eyes.

What are you both talking about so very jauntily? she says.

She says it lightly, jokily, like nothing's wrong.

Oh, you know, Patricia says. Past memories.

Old haunts, her sister says.

Jaunty haunts, Patricia says.

Ghosts you've made up rubbish about from wars that were finished over a hundred fucking years ago? Bill says.

Bill. Language, Patricia says. Be polite.

Just to be a touch more pinpoint exact on that, too, Billie, Petra says. The first of those wars ended a hundred and eight years ago and the second ended eighty one –

You're delusional. You know? Both of you. If you could hear yourselves.

Thanks, Bill, Patricia says. That's enough.

Infantile. Self indulgent. Wankers, Bill says.

Bill, Patricia says.

Bill turns to Petra.

You. You made up a horse apparition because you read about a horse in a novel.

She turns to Patricia.

As for you. I am never ever sitting in the same room watching that lame shit Four in a Bed with you again. You can't just make up stuff about real people and use them. It's offensive. No one has the right to imagine someone else. It's inauthentic. It's gross. It's immoral.

Okay, Patricia says. Calm down, Billie. Dial it down a level.

Stuck in some fictional limbo. Both of you. Like it's in any way relevant to anything real, Bill says.

Limbo. Prosthetic limbo? Petra says.

Oh, that's good, very good, Patricia says. Particularly for it being about, you know, absence. And the thing you put in place of the absence.

Bill stands up off the couch so fast it's like the couch ejected her. But then she doesn't know where to go. She turns on her heel in the middle of the room. The room spins with her.

It's you two who are the ghosts. You're so fucking insubstantial.

Now Bill is shouting.

These are some of the things she hears herself shout.

Open your eyes.

Look past yourselves.

See where we are now.

Look what's happening.

Get to the real story.

Can a person who can no longer speak still speak?
No. Obvs.
Can a horse that's been nothing but bone based fertilizer in a field somewhere for over a century come back and stand in a room?
No. Don't be stupid.
The truth, though, Bill tells herself, awake in a sleeping bag smelling of someone else on this sofa in this flat in the middle of the night, is that she herself is deluded too.
She is every bit as haunted as these two psychohystericals acting like children that she's now stuck in a flat with for the night, one of whom she has come to trust as family and will endeavour to continue to trust, even though the real revelation of family is that family is more often than not really about who isn't family.

She raged at them earlier.

She shouldn't have.

She is sorry about that now.

She will apologize to them both tomorrow.

Possibly she raged at them because the truth is she is just as hooked as they are.

Not haunted by childhood bloody mess, though. That's over. It's sorted. It happened, she survived it and she is lucky in terms of mental health stakes; unlike hundreds of thousands of people who are on waiting lists she's had longterm help and has Kayleigh the therapist to see her through if and when she needs help now. Her birth mother survived it too; all the people including herself have moved on to different possible lives from it; and her birth mother is happy in Spain, she's clean, she's well, soon she is going to have a baby and then Bill herself will have more family too.

This is all as far as Bill is concerned an excellent outcome.

No.

Bill is haunted by something related to, and every bit as shaming as – though definitely a lot more recent, so definitely way more relevant than – whatever those two women sleeping elsewhere in this flat are haunted by.

It is what she understands has really happened to the body of a real living person.

The real person is, was, a journalist.
She was a woman in her twenties. In the photos of her she had long hair and clever dark eyes. She made a name for herself by daring to go to the places other journalists were too scared or maybe too wise to go to, crossing frontlines secretly to be able to record and let people know about things nobody was ever meant to be able to report back on or say out loud or write anything about.

Bill had read about her a couple of months ago in the paper, in an article someone wrote after they found her body.

This journalist was formidable and uncompromising. She made films about and reported on what she saw and what she found out in a way that made the people she was reporting about want to kill her. So they did. They caught her. They detained her. Then when she was dead they sent her body back where she originally came from in an exchange across a border of hundreds of bodies all in bodybags.

Her bodybag was labelled Unidentified Male, as if they didn't know who or what she was.

All the same, they must've wanted someone to know this was her because they didn't burn her or get rid of the evidence. Instead they labelled her almost like it was a joke, then they left her for people to find and to have to work it out.

They also obviously wanted people to find her because on the way to killing her, and specifically because she'd been a journalist, they did some things to her body that Bill is hoping to God they did after she died and not before. They removed everything in her body that had made her a journalist: her eyes, her tongue, her brain, her vocal cords.

This is true.

This happened to a real person.

This is not just some random made up ghost story from the past.

Also, this has made Bill Wild wonder several times a day what the people who did this to her did with those body parts they removed from this person.

What did they do with her tongue?

Where are her eyes now? Did they throw her

eyes away in the trash? Did they feed them to pigs? or dogs?

Did they make soup with her brain like in some arcane story of sadism and debauchery and serve the soup to the tyrant who ordered her dead?

Did they give her vocal cords to a tyrant in a jewelled box as a birthday present?

What *would* you do, afterwards, with what you removed from someone? Not just with what you removed, but with the fact that that's what you'd done, what you did?

Bill sighs and shakes her head in the dark. She pushes herself down into the sleeping bag and she closes her eyes.

What wouldn't you do, if that theatre of savagery was what came naturally to you?

Now it is the literal inside of a dead human person's throat that is haunting Bill Wild, alive, well, here and now, sitting straight up again in the dark on a sofa, her legs crossed and her head in her hands. Specifically Bill feels them quite physically all the time, the intricate little pair of curtains made of muscle tissue on either side of the larynx that vibrate so we can say things out loud, opening for breathing, meeting in the middle for speech, singing, making any noise at all, meaningful or meaningless.

In film she's seen of vocal cords on YouTube they resemble a mouth – a second mouth. Like a mouth on its side. When they open it's like they're the wide open doorway to a tunnel or a cave you didn't know was there. When they close it's like they're kissing each other or riffing off each other, or like kids when they flap at each other's hands, something like that, she doesn't know how else to describe it. When they're wide open they look joyful, like a V, sort of like they're exclaiming upwards.

Though, ironically, at that point they're not making any noise at all, they're just letting breath openly in and out of whoever's throat they're in.

Wherever Bill is, whatever she is doing, she can feel, insistent, in her own vocal cords, the presence of the vocal cords of the girl who was the journalist.

Wild is not Bill's real surname, by the way. It's her chosen surname for now. Her birth mother's surname is Sweeper. Somewhere back in time her birth family were maybe chimney sweepers. Or road sweepers. Or mine sweepers. Cleaner-uppers of some kind. *Maintenance of public spaces*, it said somewhere online. Who knows if that's true? It sounds quite true.

She likes being more than one possible person. She likes having this choice in her of a different self or two.

She also really likes being called Wild. It's a good word to have close to her.

It keeps her wise to all the possibilities in everything, including possible savagery, keeps her high on the claws of her own toes like a fox, or a falcon on an old coat of arms, yes, on her mettle like a falcon that knows that it's being fed small stones by the person whose hand it perches on because those stones are good for it, they clean out the grease in the place in its throat called a crop, and that soon the hood'll be off and there'll be flight, and real food, something nourishing, one way or another.

Bill pushes herself down inside the sleeping bag again. There is no point in not being able to sleep. It just means you tire out easily.

The dead girl sits on the side of the sofa next to Bill.

Then she lies down along her, next to her.

The dead girl isn't there.

Dead people aren't.

Bill puts her arm round the dead girl.

Morning.

Petra and Bill are in the lounge having a passionate sounding conversation.

Because you *want* the children to be reunited at the end, Bill says.

She is still zipped into the sleeping bag. Petra is sitting next to her.

It's awful, that they aren't, she says. It's awful that it's left in mid air like that. But that's what makes you want it. That's what means you can't stop thinking about it.

Yes. We want the mother in the book to come back and find them, Petra is saying. We want to know what happened to the man the mother was with who just disappears. And we really need to know what happens to that brave girl in the end.

We don't want to be left hanging like that. I don't anyway. I really object to that.

I think that's maybe the whole point, Bill says. That whoever reads it objects to that.

I suppose it depends what someone wants from a story, Petra says. Different people will want different things. Usually I'll prefer it to have a beginning, a middle and an end. Above all, an end I'll like and not feel cheated by or left in the air by.

You want everything to be all right in the end? Bill says. You want the mystery solved?

No. Not necessarily, Petra says.

You want it to meet your needs? Take your side? You need an ending that soothes you and ties up everything neatly?

I'm just not sure that books that are novels and fiction and so on should be so close to real life, Petra says. Or so politically blatant –

But what if the point is that things like what happens in that story *are* blatantly happening in reality to real people? Bill says.

– and when I got to the end of that book I needed a lot more information, Petra says over the top of Bill. About what happened next. To the horse. To the mother. And the kids who've been separated. And all the people in that book that just, you know. Get disappeared.

What if the whole point is that the information *isn't* the point? Bill says.

Oh please, Petra says.

What if nobody *knows* what happened to them? Bill says. And what if that's the thing that makes you care?

Morning, Patricia says.

They both turn. They're flushed with talking.

Afternoon, Bill says. Did we wake you?

No, Patricia says. *They* did.

She points at the TV. A news programme is on featuring a crowd of about fifty people shouting at a building and throwing lit flares at it over a high wire fence.

We are paying for it with our taxes, a woman is saying to a camera.

She is holding a placard saying Save our kids.

Night shift report, Patricia says, I can report I was still awake at nearly 3am and I definitely saw nothing all night. No horse. I especially saw no horse at all after I fell asleep.

Coffee? Petra says. Breakfast? How'd you sleep? Because miracle of miracles, I slept well, thanks to you. Really. Thank you.

Well, you know, Patricia says. An overdue thank you to you. For watching over me enough times back in the day. I mean, back in the night.

She sits on the arm of the sofa. She pokes Bill in her side.

Two missed calls from the school's attendance secretary, she says. I'll have to call them. Then get you home.

She looks brightly at them both.

Even though I fell asleep in a chair, I don't feel at all rough. In fact it feels like I slept quite well. Who put the blanket over me and tucked it in? That was nice.

They're an army invading us, a man on TV holding a flag says. They're an army in disguise.

The flag he's holding is see through. He's holding it facing himself, broad red lines and the word England backwards.

Whose side are you on? the man is saying. Are you on the side of our women and children being safe on our streets?

All three of them watch it, hear it, exchange glances with each other.

The programme cuts to a panel in a studio.

We very much understand their frustration, a government spokesperson says. We're tackling it.

I don't get it, Bill says. How come I get taken in and put in a police station room for standing on a pavement just holding a scarf, but every politician going seems to want to be honouring the people at these protests?

The sisters look at each other in despair. Bill sees them despair. It makes fury rise inside her.

She tamps it down, for now. She tells herself this

is good energy and she will use it when she needs to, for the good. Then she laughs to herself.

Petra gets up and switches the TV off. She sighs. She goes to the kitchen. She comes back with a tray loaded with coffee, bread, jam and a bowl of spaghetti hoops.

Patricia runs a teaspoon through the spaghetti hoops.

Why did you bring me these? she says.

You like cold spaghetti hoops, Petra says. You eat them all the time.

Well, yeah. When I was ten years old, Patricia says.

That's all she'd ever eat, Petra tells Bill. Breakfast, lunch and supper.

Patricia takes a mouthful. She grimaces.

Then she eats the whole bowlful.

Right, she says. We'll need to be off soon, Bill.

A look of panic crosses Petra's face.

She's got school, Patricia says. Why don't you come back home with us for a while. Till things settle a bit.

I won't, Petra says. I'll survive. I'll be fine. But thank you. It's kind.

You can have my bedroom if you come, Bill says. I can sleep on the couch. I can lend you more novels you won't like, if you like.

She means that book you sent me, Petra tells Patricia. She liked it a bit more than I did.

I'm telling you, Bill says. It's what made a horse come and wreck her bedroom.

I tend to think something a little more factual and history based did that, Petra says.

Oh, Bill says. That reminds me.

She scrolls her phone.

Found it, she says. Listen to this. I was speaking to Jenna from school yesterday, they have a horse, they're not like horsey or rich or anything, they just have a horse. And I happened to mention your blind horse, and I asked her to ask her mother about what you have to do if you've got a horse that can't see, what the best way to look after it is, and her mother sent me some notes in an email. Right. Listening? I'll just read what she's written. So. Her mother says:

the thing to do round a horse that can't see is not to be nervous or anxious yourself or it'll sense your nervousness and it is going to feel nervous enough itself already and doesn't need your nervousness. Especially if it's just gone blind recently and had been sighted before rather than been born blind. But don't worry as it will soon settle down and although it sounds like an impossibility it is perfectly fine to have a blind horse. Blind horses are often even lovelier than seeing horses because of the bond of trust. You can lead it perfectly easily and ride it. It is the same as any other horse except it can't see. The main thing is not to put it into a herd of seeing horses that will bully it. Horses are naturally hierarchical and tribal and can be bullies just like we can. Horses are where the phrase *herd mentality* comes from.

Blind horses do tend to adapt fast to blindness though and they are already exceptionally good listeners and will become even more so if they can't see. A blind horse will always be listening for your voice to tell it what you want it to do. Always let it know you're coming towards it. You can do this by speaking to it as you approach it or by making the same sound every time you do. Soon it will know you're coming anyway because it'll be able to tell just by listening for your feet hitting the ground! It will know things about your gait that you don't know yourself. Its ears will be astoundingly discerning and its sense of smell amazing.

But it is important when you put it in a field or paddock to be sure to walk it round several times to let it know where the perimeter is. Also good if you can house it with a companion animal like a donkey or a goat or a single other good natured horse. This companion will look after it as well as keep it company. Animals are good that way. Don't use barbed wire round the field or any fencing that would hurt it if it panicked about something and ran into it. Wooden fencing is a good idea. Don't use anything sharp in the fencing. Check the ground really thoroughly and regularly for holes and stones and rubbish and fallen trees or stumps or any trip hazards at all. If there are trees you should cut their branches a bit higher than the horse's height so the horse doesn't walk into them and always take the horse where any trees that you can't move are so it knows where they are too.

And Billie above all tell your aunt not to worry. She will find she will be really close to her horse. Soon they will have a bond of trust like nothing else. It will be so much more rewarding than anyone might imagine. Big hug dear Bill from Jenna's mum Harriet.

Silence.

Aw. Thanks, Billie, Petra says. For doing that kind thing. Please thank the lady who sent it.

I'll tell her, Bill says.

Thanks, Bill, Patricia says. That was very nice of you.

A very nice thing for a niece to do, Petra says.

Yeah, Bill says. But just to make it clear, you're not my aunt yet.

What am I, then? Petra says.

You're my possible aunt, Bill says. I've got a choice here, even if you two don't.

How am I doing so far? Petra says.

Seven out of ten, Bill says.

Round about a B. That's not good enough, Petra says.

More a B plus, Bill says.

That's still not very good. What am I doing wrong? God. The youth of today are draconian beyond belief, Petra says.

We have to be, Bill says. If you're going to find yourself living in Draconia, best to speak *some* draconian. Just so you know what the signposts say.

blind horse

Now.
   Since we're talking story with beginnings, middles, ends.
   This one we're all in together:
   how would you like it to end?
   How do you imagine it will?

Here's a story, and it's one we've been telling ourselves for over two millennia.

There's a rich and powerful king, the leader of an ancient country, whose wife sends him across the sea to her homeland to bring back her sister, whom she's missing very much, for a lovely visit.

But as soon as this man meets his wife's sister he covets her. He has to have her. He has to have her as well as his wife. He is consumed by what he wants. He's got to make sure nobody else can have her, not even herself. He is so full of envy at everything and everyone that's anything to do with this young woman – her having her own life, her own voice, her own family, her own country – that he can barely contain himself.

But he acts charming in front of everybody; he performs formal statesmanship, says he's come to accompany her across the sea to visit her sister who's longing to see her.

She is pleased. She's longing to see her sister too.

He can't believe his luck when she climbs aboard his painted ship and they set off. He looks out at the ocean. Now he's got her. Now she's got no escape.

He restrains himself on the voyage; too many other people. But as soon as they land back in his kingdom he takes her to a place with high walls he's had purpose built deep in a cold dark wood in the middle of nowhere, where he shuts her up in more ways than one.

First, of course, he takes her by sheer force. He does what he likes with her.

She is broken, furious.

She shouts to the gods for help.

Then, instead, she starts shouting at him.

She tells him he'll pay for this. She tells him she's going to tell everybody her story, she'll shout from the rooftops what has happened, what he's doing and what he's done. She makes it clear to him that even if he thinks she's isolated in the middle of nowhere in some high walled prison where nobody can hear her she'll tell this truth so eloquently that trees and rocks and stones will bear witness and pass the story on.

This threat to tell the world what he's done enrages him.

So he ties her up. He removes her tongue.

(In at least one of the versions of this brutal story the tongue that the king cuts out of her mouth has a life of its own after he throws it on to the ground; it talks quietly to the earth, moves around by itself, is a creature with its own life.)

Anyway. He takes her by force again now, excited by the fact that she can't make any meaningful noise about it.

Then he leaves her in the deserted prison with a servant to see to her basic needs and goes back to his wife and his world leader life.

He pretends to be griefstricken.

He tells his wife her sister is dead, died on the voyage, and that he buried her with full honours at sea.

His wife, deep in real grief, builds an empty tomb for her sister and mourns her.

But her sister's no ghost. Locked behind those high walls she works at getting proficient at telling people things by being silent.

She persuades a servant girl to bring her a small loom. She pulls threads out of her own clothes. She makes a fine little scarf embroidered with a set of symbols that tell the story of exactly what has happened to her.

She makes sure this scarf will end up in the hands of her grieving sister.

It does.

As soon as her sister holds the scarf in her hands she understands. Now she knows.

All hell breaks loose. Plot goes mad. Atrocity follows atrocity. Everybody is full of murderousness. Blood everywhere.

A small child, an innocent, gets torn apart by his mother and his aunt, then unwittingly eaten by his father the king.

When he realizes what they've done the king lunges at the sisters to kill them both.

They grow wings. They turn into birds. One soars to the eaves of the palace, the other out of the window and off to the woods where she's the kind of bird whose song is so beautiful that poets will write about it and about her and her sister for centuries.

Not to be outdone, the king also turns into a bird.

But nobody remembers him for that.

Here's another story, albeit one not quite as ancient and off on a bit of a tangent. There aren't many stories in circulation about the outright physical flattening of individuals.

But the flattened person story is maybe connected to a set of stories we've been telling ourselves for centuries, like this one:

there was once a man renowned for his simple heart, his honesty, his contemplativeness and his quiet temperament. He travelled widely in the world converting people to his belief system. It helped that he was very good at doing things like dispelling various illnesses, dispelling devils and dispelling madness in young women who'd been chained or walled up.

When people saw that he was able to do these things they took him at his word. But his growing popularity made the people in charge – who didn't like his belief system, which wasn't the same as theirs – furious. They didn't like how powerful he seemed. They had him crucified, skinned, then decapitated.

This meant that he became sanctified, a patron saint of, among other things, leatherworkers, book binders, glove makers and butchers, also of help for skin diseases and neurological diseases. It meant, too, that in pictures portraying him he tends to have a knife in one hand and to carry over his arm the empty skin of himself, deflated, like an uncanny punctured other self, the rag of a burst balloon.

The other thing that meant he became a saint was a series of stories associated with him about miracles, stories which seemed always to be about unexpected heaviness or lightness.

The first of these stories concerns the people who killed him. They got fed up of how many mourners came and left offerings at the place his remains were kept. So they put what was left of him in a heavy lead box and threw the box into the sea.

But the box floated to the surface.

Reputedly it floated all the way to the shore of an island off Sicily. The people there found it and buried the remains of this man, whose name, it said on the box, was Bartolomeo. They built a place of worship over what was left of him and placed a large statue in there made of precious metals and dedicated to him. They also began to honour him yearly with a ritual where some strong local men carried that large statue through the streets of the town with all the townspeople following in a big procession.

One year the men who were carrying the statue found that it was a lot heavier than any of them remembered – so much so that they had to stop and put it down and rest for a bit.

They picked it up again and went on down the street.

But the statue seemed to grow even heavier. So they stopped again. They had to.

Again and again the procession through the town had to halt and the townspeople had to wait patiently while the men carrying the statue at the front let it back gently down on to the ground, looked at each other in exhausted bewilderment, got their breath back and picked it up again.

But then this happened. After another unscheduled halt in the proceedings everybody saw, further down the road, a huge section of the town wall and several high buildings behind it suddenly topple, collapse and fall in front of their eyes.

Dust rose and spread for miles.

Had the townspeople been down there, they'd all be dead.

Miracle.

Also, one year, a year in more recent memory,

an army of fascists who'd taken over the island were on the lookout for precious metals they could melt down to keep funding their ongoing invasive landgrab and regime.

They went to the place of worship and saw the statue. They nodded to each other. It was huge and surely worth a fortune.

But when they weighed it they found it weighed only a few grams, certainly not enough to be worth the trouble it'd take to melt it down.

So they put it back.

Miracle.

There happens to be a real historic massacre named after this saint with the knife and the flat skin self over his arm. One year, in France, in the sixteenth century, on his feast day in August, a group of people who hated another group of people because they had different beliefs decided they'd murder as many of the other group of people as they could. Word spread. Dead bodies littered the streets of the cities and towns and villages. Historians reckon thirty thousand people were murdered in a day.

There's also perhaps a more ancient precedent somewhere deep in this, connected to the Aztec god of earth, agriculture, goldsmiths, silversmiths and warfare, who, legend has it, decided to remove his own skin in self sacrifice to the sun to save his starving people, in a gesture towards how maize seeds lose their outer covering before they germinate, a gesture towards successful harvests.

After he did this the god went around wearing his old skin like a suit over his newly visible inner red self.

Many enslaved people lost their lives in the copycat sacrificial rituals that happened every springtime in this god's name.

End? Middle? Beginning?

There was once a man who takes the harness off a blinded horse, takes the horse by the forelock and walks it away.

It's a horse not unlike the ones kept in the stabling down the pits. When they're brought back up after a year down there they seem blinded, well, the ones that get to have the fortnight up in the light in the summer do. They don't all get it, some of them never come up. But when they do, if they do, when they bring them up and out, those horses act for a while like they can't see. Then when their eyes come back they frolic about like he doesn't know what. Well. Like horses who've been in the dark all the months when the light stops hurting their eyes again.

Jock. Joey. Harry. Bob. Prince.

Prince was a cougher. The coal dust gets to them all but got to Prince the worst. Jock was a good natured fellow, could get the lid off the snap box when no one was looking and empty it, and in the lamplight when he did that you could see it was like his eyes laughed. Harry was big. He had a rub at the top of his head between his ears that was raw and sore and hadn't been seen to, ought to have been. When he himself first came down to work the ponies, you could see the bone through Harry's shredded skin from where his head was always hitting the pit roadway ceiling. He himself was still a boy then, so small that the folds of Harry's mouth, when Harry was standing still in the stall, were level with his forehead, and he climbed up the side of the stall and treated the sore with kerosene. Then he worked with Harry and got him to know to keep his head well down till it healed. He made them make a leather halter that fitted, made them use the one that they'd been using, the wrong size for Harry, on Joey, it fitted Joey fine, so no waste. He got his mother to make a rag cushion the size of her hand and he put it under the leather against Harry's head. It got him promoted to stabling duties when he did that because they didn't want to lose Harry who was a good steady hauler and not old. Extra work but extra money, 2d per day, it all adds up, more than 4s extra a month.

This horse he's with now isn't a horse he knows.

But he can tell that it knows he knows horses and means it no harm.

Good chap, the man says. What's your name, I wonder.

He takes it down through the ruined fields and across the road towards the far trees.

The trees are a green dream.

A bird flies up. The horse hears it and doesn't startle. And another, and another. They don't startle much now, used to the guns.

The sun comes low through the branches behind them and sends all colours glancing about. He checks the ground as he goes, for anything that'll catch the horse's footing unawares, roots, rocks, boulders, dips, burrows. He tells the horse when he sees something they have to take care round. The horse, heavy, delicate, knows fine and goes with the man's voice.

Four miles now, five? The noise is still there but behind them. The man has a sense that there'll be grassland further down past these woods. He'll get the horse there first. Then he'll spy out farms, there'll be stabling, and maybe if he's lucky someone good enough to know the value of a horse, seeing or not.

Himself he can double back and live in these woods no bother for a while, a day or two, till the horse is settled where it is, then he'll go back to the boys.

He likes the way these trees creak to themselves like they're speaking their language.

Would he carve his name in them? Right now it's like they're carving themselves in him.

Green shadow accompanies the horse. Green shadow casts him too. Green shadow precedes them. It forms them both.

Front endpaper artwork (detail): Edvard Munch, *The Pathfinder*, 1912–13. Photo © Munch Museum/Rena Li